Milon and the Lion

Milon and the Lion

Jakob Streit

Floris Books

Translated by W. Forsthofer and Auriol de Smidt

Illustrations by Werner Fehlmann
First published in German under the title
Milon und der Löwe by
Verlag Freies Geistesleben in 1972.
This edition published in 2011.

British Library CIP Data available
ISBN 978-086315-841-4
Printed in Great Britain
by Page Bros Ltd

Contents

Farewell to Athens 7

On Board the *Augusta* 15

Secret Freight 19

Arrival in Stabiae 24

Shopping in Pompeii 28

Vesuvius Reigns 34

The Fall 37

The Dead City 43

The Dancing Faun 48

New Destinations 51

The Golden Titus 54

To Leptis Magna and Portus Augusti 57

Meeting Again in Rome 61

The Journey Back 65

In the Storm 68

A New Master 73

A Strange Encounter 78

The Return 83

A Change of Duties 86

The Day of the Lion Hunt 90

Betrayed and Beaten   94

The Slave Market in Alexandria   100

Arriving in Rome   104

The Great Games   111

Journey Into Freedom   119

We Meet Again in the House of Andarius   123

Last Journey with the Lion   133

Meeting in Alexandria   136

Alexandria at Night   139

Milon Collects his Guests   148

Eavesdropping   151

We Are Building   158

A Slave is Also Human   164

Homeward with Hindrances   168

With Song and Dance   173

Farewell to Athens

The rays of the late afternoon sun shone over the city of Athens on the bright temples on the hill of the Acropolis. Below, a youth ran headlong through the narrow lanes and stopped before a high, closed gate. He hammered violently upon the boards.

At the muffled banging, shuffling steps approached and a woman's voice called, "Who is this in such a hurry?"

"It's me, Tyrios! Open up for me, Agaya!"

The gate creaked open and the young man stood before the old gatekeeper, who was clearly amused at his haste.

"What's the rush? You almost knocked the gate to pieces. You're not in such a hurry with your day's work!"

"Where's Milon? I have important news for him. I know where they're taking us!"

The old servant pointed to the back garden. "Milon is picking grapes. But tell me, Tyrios, what did you find out?"

The youth didn't stop to listen. He rushed over to Milon, a slave like himself, to pass on the message. He found him in the vineyard, picking the first ripe grapes, laying them carefully in a basket. Milon was the same age as Tyrios. His tangled, dark blond hair lent a wild look to his fine features.

"Milon, we're headed for Rome! The luggage I took to Piraeus port was loaded onto a ship that sets sail tomorrow. It will cross the sea to the great city of the Romans. It's a mighty ship and it must be carrying precious cargo, for the guards wouldn't let me onto the afterdeck." Tyrios finally paused, gasping for breath after his fast run and hurried speech.

Milon offered him some grapes and asked hesitantly, "Then tonight we sleep in Athens for the last time?" Tyrios nodded vigorously, disappointed that Milon didn't seem to share his excitement.

For a moment both were silent. Tyrios took some more grapes, quenching his thirst greedily with their juice. Milon was shocked at this unexpected news from Piraeus, but he didn't show it. Without a word he glanced over the garden wall up to the hill of the Acropolis, where the bright marble temple gleamed in the dazzling sunlight.

"Tyrios," he said after a moment's silence, "would you fill this basket with grapes and carry it to Agaya? I need to go up to the temple on the Acropolis to say farewell to Alkides and to Athens."

"Aren't you even a little happy to get away from our old women? We've been running errands for them day and night! Oh Milon, soon we'll be on a ship and sailing into the wide world! The dealer said we'd be working in a noble house in Rome."

But Milon did not waver. He repeated his question: "Tyrios, please will you fill my basket?"

"Yes, go to your temples and gods! You've carried up so many loads of wood for the sacrificial fire, they should be thanking you!"

"If I'm a bit late will you calm Agaya?"

"I'll do that, as usual. She can't be upset with her favourite, Milon!"

Soon the great gate opened again and the boy slipped through, easing the hinges to close it gently behind him. The slave dealer who had bought both boys had told them not to leave the house again that day.

An agile runner, Milon made good speed through the narrow streets that led towards the Acropolis. As he climbed up the rocky hill between cypresses and olive groves, the golden evening light gleamed on the temples, making them shine radiantly like a city of the gods against the blue sky. Milon stood spellbound for a moment. He felt as though he was seeing the Acropolis in its full beauty for the first time, only now as he came to bid farewell to Athens. His heart pounded from the run, and Milon's awe and the pain of leaving mingled with its rhythmic beat. He had grown up among these columns and

buildings. Over there on that wall, he had scratched a secret sign every spring, known only to him. It showed how much he had grown over the years.

Milon moved on, instinctively slowing his pace to make the remaining time here last longer. At the final flight of steps, which led to the great halls of the Propylaea, he looked back towards the city in the fading light. The sea, which tomorrow would carry him into an unknown future, glittered in the distance. He climbed the last steps up to the mighty columns, paying no attention to the passers-by. He reached out to touch a pillar that had soaked up the day's heat, sliding both hands upwards along its grooves. He pressed his forehead against the warm stone, closed his eyes and whispered faint words, hardly knowing what he was saying.

Suddenly Milon heard his name being called. Startled, he turned from the pillar to face a tall figure in a white robe. It was Alkides, the young priest who had befriended Milon when he had first come to serve as a wood carrier for the sacrificial fire, under his master's orders, three times a week.

"Are you sad, Milon? You're late. The evening sacrifice is over. Come with me back into town."

"Honourable Alkides, I am sold. This is my last visit to the Acropolis ... to say goodbye. Tomorrow I will leave Greece by ship ... a Roman trader ... Italy!"

Astonished, the young priest looked at Milon and took his arm. "How is this possible? What happened to make your master give you away so suddenly? Have you angered him?"

"No, noble Alkides. My master accidentally fell from a horse and was killed on a journey to Eleusis. His wife, my mistress, is selling the house and slaves and will live with her son in Olympia. Tyrios and I were bought yesterday by a Roman."

Milon's head sank as he spoke and Alkides saw the despair on the face of his young friend, who had so often taken on the lowly work of preparing the sacrifice. He understood how hard this farewell to Athens must be for him. Alkides thought for a moment before saying, "Come, Milon, let's go to the temple of the Goddess and beg a farewell blessing for you."

Together they climbed the last steps towards the entrance gate. The columned hall glowed red in the evening light as they both walked silently towards the Parthenon temple. Alkides raised his arms in the entrance hall and said a prayer for Milon. Afterwards they sat outside on the top step of the temple, at the foot of one of the great pillars, the glowing disc of the sun-chariot sinking before them.

"Tell me," asked Alkides, "how were you sold into Roman lands so far away? Couldn't they find a new master for you here in Athens?"

"Yesterday my mistress's son came with a trader from Piraeus. He buys young Greek slaves to sell in Rome. His ship is waiting in the harbour ready for departure. He must have offered good prices because Tyrios and I were sold on the spot. Slaves have no choice in what happens to them. We'll be collected first thing tomorrow morning. I'm afraid of the Romans. I've heard that the she-wolf is their sign. They say almost all nations of the earth bow down to them. Alkides, you must know about the Romans? Maybe you can ease my fear?" Milon looked at the priest as if his whole future depended on his words.

"Young friend," Alkides began, "I would have been happier for you to stay in Athens. Better a slave in Athens than a free man in Rome, we say! In Greece we see the Romans as our conquerors. We have to pay tribute to them. The favour of the gods left us when they defeated us. They've copied our temples in Rome, robbed our images of the gods and set them up there. Our service to the gods is nothing but an empty superstition to them.

"But don't be afraid, Milon; since the goddess of fate guides your journey to Rome, go with confidence. Wherever you are, the sacrificial fires you celebrated here at the altar with us will continue to burn for you. Let the image of the temples and columns of the Acropolis stay upright within you. If you ever feel distressed then close your eyes and let the vision of these temples of Athens shine inside you. Courage and faith will become strong in your heart because, above all humanity, the eternal gods prevail."

Alkides paused for a moment and brought out a bronze coin imprinted with the head of the goddess Athena from the folds of his robe.

"Here, Milon, take this as a memory, then you will always carry a part of Athens with you."

Milon took the gift and pressed it against his heart as if he held a great treasure.

"Thank you, Alkides. You've made my goodbye harder and easier at the same time. I will remember that the same sun shines over Athens and Rome and the same stars circle around our wide earth."

"Yes, that's true," agreed Alkides. "You'll not be disheartened in a foreign land with them watching over you. Now, let's walk down to the city together, and say goodbye as we go. Look over there — the evening star! That's the heavenly body of the goddess Aphrodite. She shines over the sea! It's a good omen for your journey!"

When Milon returned home he found the gate unlocked. Softly he pushed it open, but Agaya was waiting for the runaway, and noticed the quiet creak. He heard her trembling voice. She rushed out of the house and as soon as she saw Milon, tears came to her eyes.

"Tyrios has already gone to Piraeus. The Roman dealer was here and wanted to take you to the ship too."

Shocked, Milon said, "But he ordered us for tomorrow morning. Why the sudden hurry?"

Agaya pressed his fingers between her old rough hands and said, "Milon, the dealer was very angry when he couldn't find you. He will whip you tomorrow morning when you arrive late at the ship. Listen! Don't go to Piraeus; don't go to the Romans. Leave Athens secretly; flee into the mountains to my brother, who grazes his sheep above Delphi. No one will search for you there. You know the way. There you'll be safe. You can be a shepherd again, as you were as a little boy. Later, when this is all forgotten, you'll return to Athens as a free man!"

Agaya moved her lips, shaking as she gazed anxiously at the young man, waiting for his agreement. In the silence Milon looked over the garden wall towards the star shining above the sea. He heard Alkides' farewell words: "The star of Aphrodite, a good omen for your journey!"

Yes, he had said goodbye to Athens. He wanted to go the

way of destiny with Tyrios across the sea to Rome. He stroked Agaya's white hair, held her head between his hands and said firmly, "Agaya, the world is opening before me! I will board the ship tonight and sail with the Roman she-wolf. Dear Agaya, you've always been a mother to me. I'll never forget you even in faraway lands. Go sometimes to the Acropolis and pray for me at the Parthenon."

He took his hands away and continued, "I'll quickly tie my things in the travel cloth you gave me and go to the Roman ship now, so I don't anger the dealer too much."

Although Agaya sobbed quietly, she knew that Milon had made his decision, so she helped him pack his modest belongings, adding fruit and honey bread.

Milon opened the gate, casting his long shadow on the cobbled lane outside. Agaya raised the lamp to light his young face, engraving the picture in her memory for the last time. She laid one hand tenderly on his shoulder. He had been like a son to her for these last seven years.

"I'll come down to the sea early tomorrow morning to bless your journey," she said firmly. Milon didn't argue so she added, "I'll find your ship. Look out for me. It will bring you good luck!"

Milon had a long way to go through the darkness to reach the sea. Being a light-footed runner, he soon reached the broad road that connected the city of Athens with the port. Donkey carts and loaded mules were still busy bringing goods from the harbour up to the city.

Suddenly, behind him, Milon heard the rattle of a larger vehicle: a noble carriage drawn by a pair of horses and lit by four runners bearing torches. *A good chance to keep up,* thought Milon, running close behind the carriage where he could move a lot faster, following the glow of the torches. He suddenly felt full of happiness, as if the lights were there to guide him. Once again he saw the evening star glittering over the sea before him. With Athens behind him, he was running into a new life! The trotting of hooves on the cobblestones fired his limbs with exhilaration. Jubilation charged his rapid breath. Again and again he leapt high into the air. He forgot his slavery, which hadn't been oppressive up to now under the care of good Agaya. He forgot that Rome bore the sign of the she-wolf. Before him lay unknown distant shores, and within him courage to venture into the world.

On Board the *Augusta*

The harbour life of Piraeus was still bustling when Milon reached the dark shore, searching for the Roman ship. Crews were returning to their ships from wine houses. Two drunken men staggered along, swearing through the darkness. Flickering torches lit up faces for an instant. How could Milon find the ship in the dark without even knowing its name?

A torch-bearer approached him and Milon asked, "Can you tell me where to find the ship which departs for Rome tomorrow?"

The elderly seaman answered, "The Roman ships usually leave from the front of the harbour because they're bigger than the fishing boats, which moor here at the back. Go further forward."

So Milon moved seaward, walking slowly to avoid the many stones, poles and ropes. Soon a group of men with torches came up behind him. *I'll follow them*, thought Milon.

As the group passed, it struck him how silently these young people were walking. They were a group of slaves with luggage, probably up to thirty of them. Suddenly he noticed Tyrios among them, who he'd thought would already be on the ship. He rushed over and whispered, "Tyrios, I am here!"

Tyrios turned his head and a flicker of joy lit up his face. "Milon," he whispered, "the gods be thanked that you have come! Stay close to me. The dealer is following with the supervisors just behind us. He's furious because you and two others couldn't be found. Tomorrow morning he'll send for the missing ones. The ship can't sail without them because the price has already been paid."

"So I'll walk with you now and sneak in with you all together?"

"You can't do that," said Tyrios, "our names have been written down on a wax tablet. But as soon as we reach the ship we'll go to the dealer. We had a long wait in town at the market place

15

until we were all brought together. Look out, we're close to the ship. The first torch-bearers have stopped."

A wide-beamed ship loomed out of the dark, sparsely lit by the torch flames. Calls were heard and a ladder was lowered. The group of slaves began to climb up the tilted beams into the belly of the ship, while a supervisor marked the name of each one on a wax tablet.

"Now's the time," said Tyrios to Milon. "I'll come with you to report to the dealer and the captain."

They moved inconspicuously to the back of the group. Tyrios and Milon stepped towards the trader, who was dressed in Roman fashion, and Tyrios greeted him humbly. "Noble lord," he said, "here is my companion from the house of Midias, who was out on an errand when you came to collect us. He has come swiftly to Piraeus and asks your pardon for his delay."

In true slave fashion Milon threw himself at the feet of his new master. The merchant was so astonished by the Greek courtesy and Tyrios' mastery of language, that he forgot to draw the leather whip from his belt. He said, "And where are the other two?"

Promptly Tyrios replied, "I know nothing about them."

"Damned fellows," hissed the dealer. "Let that one go to be registered." With a gesture of his hand they were dismissed.

Relieved, they hurried up the ladder with the last of the slaves. From the deck of the ship they climbed down rough steps into the ship's hold.

There a naked wooden floor and yawning darkness awaited the slaves for their night's rest. Their bundles of clothing had to serve as pillows. Tyrios and Milon held hands so they didn't lose each other while they searched for a space. Every second step they stumbled over a body, with the occasional blow of a fist or a muttered curse. Finally everyone was settled, higgledy-piggledy across the floor, and the talking and swearing subsided. Soon the first snores resounded through the air, which was thick with the odour of perspiration and pitch.

"Our journey begins in the underworld," Milon whispered to Tyrios. "The only thing missing is Cerberus, the hell hound,

16

with his three heads and serpent tail!" The dark and difficult situation had not eroded their humour.

Milon fumbled two pieces of honey bread out of his bundle and gave one to his companion. "Here, take some ambrosia to remind you that Hades has not yet swallowed us!"

After a while Tyrios whispered, "Milon, were you able to read the letters written on the ship? You learnt the Greek and Roman signs with Alkides, didn't you?"

"Yes, I saw them but I'm not sure what they mean. The ship is called *Augusta*. Maybe it's the name of a Roman goddess, come to guide us from Hades to Elysium, the world of the blessed."

The waves slapped monotonously against the sides of the ship; soon sleep spread her mantle over weary slave eyes.

Early the next morning, Piraeus was filled with the hustle and bustle of a busy port. With the first dawn, a supervisor had gone ashore with two helpers to collect the missing slaves from Athens. When they returned with them, the sun stood high over the horizon. A favourable breeze was blowing, billowing the raised foresail out towards the sea. The two latecomers climbed the ship's ladder in chains, and were welcomed with whiplashes. The captain snorted with anger and ordered that they be bound in the ship's dark hold for the duration of the voyage. Milon shuddered at the thought that he could have been the third on the chain. Full of compassion he watched the poor boys climb down the ladder into darkness.

As always when a big ship prepared to depart, a curious crowd gathered. Calls rang out and commands were given to loosen the mooring ropes. The rigging was already rattling when a gaunt old woman dressed in black came running up. She stopped alongside the ship and began to pour oil from a small clay flask into the water, murmuring half-sung words. She beat conjuring signs into the air and over the water. She asked the god of the wind to be a good escort. The consecrated oil she had poured was an offering to the sea god Poseidon for his mercy, that he might grant them a storm-free voyage.

She took a few steps back from the edge, shading her eyes

from the bright morning sun, and called up with a shrill voice, "Milon! Milon!"

Out of the crowd on board stepped a youth. He climbed nimbly to a man's height up the back mast and waved a light-coloured cloth, fluttering it to and fro above his head. The last sail was raised, the anchor weighed, and the *Augusta* glided softly out towards the open sea.

The old woman ran along the harbour wall after the ship crying, "Oh Milon, Milon, where will they take you? Your Agaya will never see you again."

She could no longer see the white cloth or hold back her tears. Agaya sat down on a tangle of ships' ropes and sobbed quietly to herself. Each time she lifted her head and looked out to sea, the *Augusta* looked smaller.

A fisherwoman passing by with a leather bag of fish to sell in Athens recognised the old woman as one of her customers and stopped to ask, "Agaya, what are you doing weeping here in Piraeus? Can your feet not carry you home any more? Come with me, Agaya. We're going the same way."

Ashamed to be seen crying, and calmed a little by the fisherwoman's kind words, the old lady stood up. "I came with our boys Milon and Tyrios to the ship," she explained. "For seven years I've raised Milon like my own child. Now our mistress has sold him to Rome. He journeys away there on that ship. I've grown old serving my master, but now that he's dead I'll go back to Delphi where I come from, to my brother."

As they turned to leave, Agaya added, "Wait. I'm glad to return to Athens with you. But first let me fill my bottle with some of the seawater on which Milon is journeying so far away. I'll wrap my hands around it in prayer each day." She moved towards the harbour edge, dipped in the flask and tucked it under her arm as a precious reminder.

And so Agaya wandered with the fisherwoman towards Athens. From time to time she stopped to look back at the fading shimmer of the sailing ship, until it dissolved in the last glitter of the waves.

Secret Freight

For days, the *Augusta* sailed with fair winds around the shores of the Peloponnes. Milon and Tyrios, together with some other slaves, were taught to climb the masts and ropes, to raise the sails or furl them when the wind changed. This gave them access to the guarded afterdeck, where large, mysterious bundles lay, wrapped in cloths tied with ropes. Nobody knew what was hidden inside. The slaves had different suspicions, but everyone agreed that it was precious loot, which the Romans were taking from Greece. After all, imperial soldiers guarded it day and night.

One night, as Tyrios and Milon were lying on their wooden planks below deck, Tyrios whispered to his friend, "The moon is so bright I can't sleep. Shall we sneak to the afterdeck to find out what the secret freight is, hidden in those bundles? I'm dying to know what we're carrying across the sea."

Milon nodded and whispered, "We could climb up through the helmsman's hatch at the rear of the ship. But he sits at the helm through the night, so he might notice us."

"First, one of us should look through the hatch and watch him for a while," said Tyrios. "During the day, when the wind is calm, he often wanders around and sits with the guard. Come on, Milon, let's go on our first adventure. My hair is dark, so I can poke my head though the hatch without much danger of being seen."

Tyrios crawled from his sleeping place towards the back of the ship, followed by Milon. The boards of the ship creaked constantly, so no one paid attention to the small sounds they made as they felt their way forward. A faint glimmer showed where the helmsman's hatch opened. Tyrios lifted his body and Milon watched as he swung himself up.

After a short while Tyrios lowered his head back down through the opening and whispered, "Come up! The helmsman's further down with the guard!"

Milon pulled himself up and they crouched on deck in the cool night air. The guard and helmsman were sitting further down the deck chatting, so there seemed to be no danger in them exploring the treasures. Sliding, they eased themselves between the enormous bundles and began to loosen the tightly knotted ropes, which held leather hides and fabric around the hidden objects. Now and again Tyrios looked up to check that the helmsman and guard were still distracted.

Milon had chosen a longish sack, which they began to untie. When at last they uncovered a protruding curved edge, they almost cried out. In the light of the moon they saw the serene, white face of a marble statue — a divine woman.

"Aphrodite," Milon whispered, "covered in filthy cloths, stolen and taken away by the Romans!"

He was deeply moved by the beauty of her moonlit face. Lost in thought, he stroked the cold stone. He remembered seeing Aphrodite, the goddess of beauty, in a small temple in Athens, surrounded by pillars and with flowers at her feet. Compassion, pain and anger welled up in him as he saw the image of the goddess degraded in this way.

Meanwhile, Tyrios had managed to push one hand underneath the covers of another bundle. "Here, too, there's a head, an arm. This ship is full of stolen gods. I've heard that the Roman Emperor loves to put statues of gods in the gardens of his palaces."

For a while, the two stared silently at the shimmering marble statue of the goddess, which Milon had now completely freed, as she looked up at the night stars. "Aphrodite must remain in Greece," Milon said into the soft rush of the waves. "What do you think, Tyrios, are we strong enough to throw her overboard into the sea here at the shores of Greece without anyone noticing? Then no Roman can defile her with his mocking stare."

"I'm with you!" Tyrios whispered. "But there'll be trouble if they catch us!" Dexterous as a cat, Tyrios crawled between the covered figures and soon returned, saying, "They're both lying on sheepskins sharing their wine jug, laughing, grunting and talking nonsense. Let's try."

The statue was not quite as tall as a real person. The two lads were strong and they managed to raise it without much trouble, placing sheets underneath to prevent the noise of stone scraping on wood. Tyrios threw some of the filthy covers overboard. For him, this was a welcome mischievous adventure. For Milon, this divine image was truly sacred, and he was doing an important deed for Greece and her gods: to hand Aphrodite over to the sea on the shores of the Peloponnes. He remembered what Alkides had told him about the goddess of beauty; how she had emerged from the foaming tides of the ocean and inspired Greek artists to create beautiful works.

"You came from the Greek tides and to Greek tides you will return!" Milon whispered to her.

As the white marble goddess stood in all her beauty in the moonlight, swaying slightly from side to side with the ship, Milon nearly sank down before her in devotion, but he was afraid that Tyrios would mock him. Carefully, half pushing, half turning, every sound muffled by the sheets, they manouevred her to the edge of the ship. Gently they tipped the figure over the rail.

For a moment she lay horizontal before dropping down towards the dark waves. But as they eased the statue over the edge, the marble pedestal on which she stood struck the wooden planks. To the boys' horror a loud crash rang through the ship. The guard and helmsman sprang up and hurried to the afterdeck, following the noise. Tyrios pulled Milon quickly down, and they crawled into the darkness between the other bundles. In a flash Tyrios spread a sheet from the goddess over himself and his friend.

The guard and helmsman moved nearer until they stood so close that they could have touched their feet. The guard said anxiously, "What on earth could have made that noise? It sounded as if a mast had broken, yet there's no wind."

The helmsman replied, "No man could have made that noise. Maybe one of the stone figures tipped over. But the waves would have to be much stronger, and they're all lying here like ... By Orcus! What's this? An empty space! Wasn't one of the statues here? This place is haunted! It's gone! I'll fetch a light, we must look closer."

The frightened guard said, "I'll come with you, something uncanny has happened here!"

The men hurried away to the lower deck, where two hanging lamps were always burning. Tyrios and Milon disappeared through the helmsman's hatch, not forgetting to throw the remaining cloths overboard to hide any trace of what they'd done.

Their hearts raced as they lay safe below deck. Tyrios, excited after their daring venture, cheerfully dug his friend in the ribs with his fist and elbow. When Milon's heartbeat calmed, he was filled with joy because they had saved the goddess.

Two figures with a swaying lantern wandered around up on the afterdeck for some time, shining their light into every corner, only to stop again at the empty space from which the goddess had escaped.

Looking timidly around, the guard whispered, "I think Aphrodite lay here. She was exceedingly precious. She's gone and she won't come back! I feel uneasy about this journey. I've often crossed the sea with corn, oil, wine or wood, but never with images of the gods. It's bad luck for our journey to Italy."

The helmsman added, "By Orcus and hell's dog Cerberus, that's strange. Who knows, they might all disappear from under the sheets, one every night! I already fear for tomorrow night. Let's go back to the foredeck, the helm is fastened and needs no attention. Come, keep the lamp burning! I'll fill a fresh jug with wine."

"Okay," said the guard, "but promise me you won't tell anyone. I mean, one goddess doesn't really matter — surely no one will notice. Help me carry that wooden bench over here to fill the empty space, then even the captain won't notice

Aphrodite's flight. And when they take the sheets off in Rome, we'll know nothing."

And so it was. A crudely made bench filled the space where Aphrodite had lain. Shabby sailcloths, which were sometimes hoisted when the wind blew mildly, were placed over it, and no one noticed the flight of the goddess.

Arrival in Stabiae

The *Augusta* sailed with fair winds across the stormless sea. As they approached the island of Sicily and prepared to sail through the straits of Messina, everyone looked up at the high mountain on the island. An enormous pillar of smoke billowed from its peak, even though the sky was clear.

Tyrios heard the captain say to one of the supervisors, "Earth's deep fires are restless. Brave Vulcanus forges in the underworld." Milon stood, absorbed, watching the smoking mountain. Tyrios came up to him and repeated the words he'd heard, but not understood.

"Well, I can only say what I know from Alkides," said Milon. "Hephaestus, who the Romans call Vulcanus, is the blacksmith of the gods. He lives in the fires of the earth. This mountain must be a holy shrine of his. We're following the voyage of Odysseus, who also came this way."

Soon the coastal strip of Italy appeared on the right. As the *Augusta* sailed through the straits, Milon felt as though he was sailing into a new life. An ocean lay between him and his homeland. The gateway to the Roman Empire was opening before him on the deep, blue surface of the sea.

Milon was ordered to untangle ropes and knots, and soon Tyrios reappeared. Full of curiosity, he was good at creeping up on people and listening in to their conversations. It was his task to pour water and wine for the Roman crew, so he went everywhere and got to hear things that wouldn't normally reach the ears of slaves. When he appeared at Milon's side with a knowing expression on his face, Milon knew that his friend had news.

"Milon," he whispered with excitement, "I've just heard something. The captain said to the helmsman. The winds have been favourable so tomorrow we'll arrive at the port of Stabiae. The owner of the *Augusta* lives there and he will check our ship and its cargo. His name is Pomponianus and he's as rich as a prince. He owns many ships and lives in a villa near the sea. He must be close to Caesar, since we're carrying imperial freight on board."

Milon wasn't sure whether to be pleased with this news. He was afraid because the uncertain life of a Roman slave would soon begin. He might even be separated from Tyrios, his closest friend, so he answered, "Tyrios, you're so good at dealing with our masters. I could bear our slavery in Rome much better if you could keep us together."

"I'll try, Milon. I can't imagine why we'd be separated," said Tyrios. "I hope this Pomponianus doesn't notice the missing statue of Aphrodite. He might get angry and sell us all as rowers on a galley; that'd be the end of us. Milon, the day after tomorrow we might be in Rome!"

The following morning the ship bustled with activity. The captain shouted orders. Everything had to be clean and tidy. Patched or dirty sails were replaced and the deck was scrubbed. The slaves were ordered to wash themselves and tie clean cloths around their loins. When the ship finally called at Stabiae, everything was ready to receive Pomponianus.

As the great master descended the steps from his villa to the ship with his attendants, both the crew and the lined-up slaves were ordered to call out three times, "Vivat Pomponianus!" On board, the captain handed him three parchment rolls. The slaves were listed on one of them, the goods on another and on the third the secret freight.

When the master had inspected the slaves and congratulated the trader on finding so many young people to be sold in Rome for high prices, he went into the ship's hold to look at the barrels of oil and wine. Lastly, he and his attendants sat down on the afterdeck where the statues were kept.

The captain had told Tyrios to wait there with cups and a jug of sweet Greek wine to offer to Pomponianus and his attendants when they entered the afterdeck. Tyrios had taken Milon as his helper. While Milon filled the cups, Tyrios offered them to the visitors and bowed gracefully before Pomponianus and his attendants, just as he'd learned to do in Athens. The visitors enjoyed the wine and Milon kept the cups filled.

Suddenly the great master pointed to the hidden statues and demanded to see one of them. When the ropes were untied and the cloths taken off, a statue of a faun appeared, the upper half human and the lower half goat, with one leg raised for dancing. He held a flute to his mouth.

Pomponianus, merry from all the wine, roared with laughter, "I will not give this fellow to the Roman Emperor! He will remain in Stabiae and go into my garden. He can blow his flute for the fish to dance in my pond!"

Eagerly, the captain had the figure wrapped again and carried to the edge of the ship to be unloaded. Using ropes, planks and poles, strong slaves carried the bundle on land and up to the villa. Others followed with a barrel of Greek wine. This entertaining spectacle kept Pomponianus busy, so he didn't check the list of statues or notice that the statue of Aphrodite had vanished.

Before leaving the ship, Pomponianus asked the captain for one or two young slaves to keep as servants. He had noticed the two serving wine. They had pleased him and he would take them straight away. And so it came that Tyrios and Milon walked up the steps among the attendants of the train of dignitaries. They carried their few belongings in bundles on their backs.

When he reached the terrace, Pomponianus turned to watch the ship's departure. Sails raised, flag waving, the ship set sail towards Rome. Tyrios whispered to Milon, "I want to go with them. What a pity we didn't stay hidden on the ship."

Milon replied, "But this master seems good natured, and the city over there at the foot of the mountain reminds me of Athens. I think I could live here. I have a strange feeling about Rome, a fear I can't explain."

Just then a fat little man approached the two newcomers and spoke to them in Greek, "Now, my fellows, I'm your supervisor.

I was also born in Greece. Call me Fuscus. From today you will be learning the Roman language. I will tell you what to do. If you're hard working and well behaved, you will have a good time. If you're lazy and stubborn, we have pliable Roman whips."

When Fuscus spoke he rolled his eyes in such a way that they could hardly hide their laughter. But Tyrios quickly said, "Venerable Fuscus, we will try hard to satisfy you. But please tell me, what is the name of that great city over the river?"

"What! You don't know Pompeii, the blossom of the Roman cities? Sixteen years ago part of it was destroyed by an earthquake, but it has risen again — even more beautiful than before."

Fuscus was talkative, thanks to the sweet Greek wine. "In the next few days we'll go shopping in Pompeii, and you can come as carriers. You'll be amazed at what there is in Pompeii: shops, workmen and wine taverns. Twenty thousand souls live in the city!"

In the meantime, the master had led the faun carriers to the pond, where magnificent fish swam in an artificial stone basin. The statue was released from its cloths and put up on a wall at the edge of the pool. It's reflection danced on the gently rippling surface. Pomponianus was delighted with his find: this animal-human figure who stood grinning on one foot playing his flute.

Milon said to Tyrios, "Well, I'm glad it's not Aphrodite standing here being gawked at by Romans. This faun suits them much better; they seem to take life as an easy gamble too." *Perhaps there are shining fish admiring Aphrodite as she sleeps in the Ionian tides*, he thought.

Tyrios pulled Milon's arm and woke him from his dreams. "Come, Fuscus is waving. He's rolling his eyes again. He wants to give us work."

Shopping in Pompeii

More than two weeks had passed in service to the rich Pomponianus, and it was nearly the end of the hot month of August. The newcomers had come to respect their friendly older master. With Fuscus and a gardener, they had built a higher wall for the faun at the fishpond, and no day went by without Pomponianus resting under a shady tree nearby. Serving in the house and garden was pleasant, if a little boring after Athens and their voyage. Often they would look across to Pompeii and the mountain of Vesuvius lying beyond it. They were still waiting for an opportunity to see the city.

At last the day came when Fuscus announced, "Today we'll go to Pompeii. The four youngest fellows will row the boat. Our master will come too. Fetch baskets and jugs, there are all sorts of things to buy."

Tyrios and Milon were among the youngest. Down below at the river Sarnus they boarded the four-manned rowing boat that Pomponianus used for journeys to Pompeii. It was colourful, with gilded wooden carvings at the bow. From the conversation between Fuscus and Pomponianus they learnt that some houses in Pompeii had been damaged the day before by a slight earthquake, which was felt in Stabiae too.

The mouth of the river Sarnus opened into the sea close to Pompeii. It had been enlarged to serve as a port where, after a short crossing, they moored the boat and got out.

Pomponianus commanded, "Once you've finished shopping in the city, Fuscus, return here with the youngsters. But have a bath at the hot springs. It may be several hours before I return from visiting my friends." The master went on his way alone, and Fuscus took the four boys with him.

As they left the river port, Milon watched the fishing boats and small cargo ships. He was particularly impressed by the gilded rowing boats, which belonged to the rich citizens of Pompeii.

They entered the inner city through a tall gate. Compared to the streets of Athens, the Pompeiian streets seemed very narrow. They had to jump onto the almost knee-high pavement when a carriage approached. Shops opened onto the streets, and everywhere workmen were busy at their benches. Leather was sewn and made into belts and shoes. In a metal workshop copper was being hammered, and in the windows, the most beautiful buckles and brooches, rings and necklaces were displayed. Innkeepers with huge stone jugs poured red and golden wine into drinking bowls and offered it with bread and roast chicken or baked fish. There were oil lamps in various sizes to buy, and next to those, amidst a mass of vases and pots, sat a potter-woman, loudly advertising her wares. A busy trader waved colourful scarves through the air, handing them eagerly to curious ladies who tried them on.

At a well, poorer women, whose houses had no piped water, gathered with jugs and buckets. Milon heard them complaining about the damage from yesterday's earthquake. One of them pointed fearfully towards the cloud of smoke which hung over Mount Vesuvius.

Donkey carts carried fruit and vegetables from the countryside to be spread on cloths in the market hall. Fuscus had his jug filled with fish sauce at one of the stalls, and at another he bought flour. Milon's basket was filled with eggs, carefully layered between vine leaves. Tyrios carried two heavy jugs with oil from an oil mill.

When Fuscus and the youngsters arrived at the wide square of the forum, he allowed them to put down their loads and have a look at the temples and other buildings. Broken stones lay here and there after yesterday's earthquake. A crack gaped from the top to bottom of a wall of the city hall. Milon wasn't surprised to find Greek pillars in the temples; Alkides had told him how the Romans had adopted them.

Fuscus waved them over to a shady place near the market hall and said, "Put everything here on the ground while I go to the bathhouse. You two newcomers may have a look around the city. Vesonius and Vargo, stay here with the goods and rest until I return."

So Milon and Tyrios set out on a tour of discovery, strolling through the busy streets. They admired the beautifully painted house façades, unlike any they had seen in Athens. Out of one of the houses came a crowd of richly dressed people, the ladies in gold and silver jewellery and colourful scarves. High-spirited laughter resounded from the walls. The two friends stepped back into a corner to watch the stream of happy people. Children with small baskets threw flowers over a couple as they stood in the doorway. The stone pavement was carpeted in blossoms.

"Oh, a wedding!" cried Tyrios. "I'd like to be a bridegroom, with such wealth and happiness."

The procession moved on towards the forum. As they passed, the fragrance of scented water floated from their garments. Tirelessly the children strewed flowers from their baskets. One rose fell at Tyrios' feet. Quickly he picked it up and breathed in its scent. Then he turned to Milon. "Poor devils we are. It would be amazing to be rich!"

"There are poorer ones than we," Milon replied. "Look how cripples and wretched beggars follow the procession to pick up a copper coin here and there."

They watched for a while longer before continuing their adventure. They reached a narrow street where the smell of fresh bread wafted towards them, and they noticed a peculiar crunching sound, which got louder as they approached. Around the corner of a house, they saw a strange sight: men stood at tall stone cylinders turning handles.

"They're mills!" Milon exclaimed. "Look down below at the white flour!" Four of the millers were resting, while a fifth poured fresh corn in from above.

Tyrios asked, "How long do you turn these monsters for?"

"From dawn till dusk. The Pompeiians eat mountains of bread!"

Behind these mills was the baker, who was taking steaming loaves of bread out of a huge stone oven, which his helper piled in different baskets according to size.

"I'll buy a small one," Tyrios said. He took a coin from his belt and exchanged it for a fresh loaf of bread.

Where on earth did he get that money? Milon thought. *There's always something in his belt!*

Eagerly Tyrios shared the bread, saying, "This fresh Pompeiian bread is delicious, but you might burn your mouth as you bite off a piece!"

Chewing the bread, they turned towards the forum to wait for Fuscus to return from the bathhouse. Milon stopped in front of a wall across a square. On the limestone plaster, painted in red, he read an inscription and he suddenly roared with laughter. Tyrios, who couldn't read, asked, "What's so funny? Do the Pompeiians write jokes on their houses?"

"Look here, you can see two different inscriptions. The upper one, big and beautifully written, announces that, 'Soon in the arena the famous gladiator Satrius Valens will fight. Until now, an invincible favourite of the gods, he has conquered every enemy.' Underneath it, written in clumsy letters a second inscription says, 'It's a miracle, o wall, that under the weight of this written nonsense you do not fall!' That must have been added by an enemy of Satrius Valens to make him look ridiculous. I'd like to see these two fighting in the arena! They must be wrestlers."

In the meantime, the warm bread eaten, they reached the forum and strolled along its columned halls. Milon saw a few elegant youths sitting on shady steps. In front of them sat a lecturer who was obviously teaching them.

Milon said to Tyrios, "Let's sneak behind the pillars so we can hear what they're learning!"

"I'm not interested. I'll go back to the market hall to the others. Fuscus might be back soon. *Vale*, Milon!"

Pompeii must have impressed him, thought Milon, *he suddenly said goodbye in Roman!*

He sneaked up to the steps behind one of the tall pillars. The lecturer was reciting a story to his pupils about the Romans' fight against barbarians. "We Romans are called upon to subject all the peoples of the earth to our rule. A nation who obeys Rome is like a ship that has returned from the wild sea to the harbour. Rome was chosen by the gods to rule the earth. Every Roman must know that this is our pride, our daily thought: the great, eternal Rome!"

Milon had heard enough. He strolled along the columned hall towards the temple of Apollo, where he was greeted by Greek pillars. A group of traders were haggling with each other on the forecourt. Beggars hung wretchedly around the steps, some playing dice and shouting. Women walked about offering wine and food and baskets for sale. Behind the chaos, the slim pillars reminded him of the Acropolis. But in Athens everyone approached the temple respectfully; no one would have dared to drink, play dice or trade in front of a temple.

Suddenly he heard the clang of bronze and two fat priests appeared on the steps to announce the beginning of the sacrifice. Only a few people rose lazily from the crowd. Curiosity led Milon towards the temple. He would have liked so much to glimpse the inner chamber, to catch sight of the form of Apollo from the distance. He was lucky. The two tall doors stood open. He went a bit closer. Out of the half-dark shimmered a white marble figure. It was a wonderful Greek statue of the god, which the Romans had kidnapped from Greece. Now Apollo stood in there, trapped in the darkness, forgotten in the business of the street.

"Away with you, wretched slave!" commanded the voice of a temple servant. A fist struck him in the side. Milon staggered between the pillars and sprang quickly down the steps back to the forum.

When he arrived back with his companions, they were worrying; Fuscus could be back at any moment.

Suddenly, what was that? They heard a muffled rumbling. Milon and Tyrios, who were sitting on the edge of a fountain, felt a shudder pass beneath them. They heard shouting and the earth shook. People rushed out of houses. Women left their stalls and hurried towards the temples, where they thought they would be on consecrated ground. The shaking grew stronger — mayhem. Through the muffled rolling of the earth and screams of the people, came the crash of falling stones as they broke off the façades of buildings.

Fuscus ran back, calling to the slaves, "Quick! Escape to the ship! Away to the harbour!"

It wasn't easy to get through the panicked crowd in the packed lanes. A fat innkeeper dashed out of a house, knocking Milon and his egg basket over. Back on his feet, Milon glanced at the yellow egg trail on the pavement. *Who cares about eggs*, he thought, *this is a matter of life and death!* Milon had lost his companions and had to fight through to the harbour alone. But he wouldn't let go of the basket, no matter how often it held him back.

At last he arrived at the harbour. Fuscus and the other three had prepared the boat for departure, but the master wasn't there. Worried sailors pushed their boats away from the bank, setting out towards the open sea. Here and there wild fleeing figures leapt into boats as they pulled away. Waiting was a test of patience for Fuscus and the four slaves. But it was impossible to go in search of Pomponianus.

At last he appeared, breathless, his face so covered in sweat and dust that they could hardly recognise him. Suppressing his fear with masterful calm, he ordered, "Cast off! Row away!"

Vesuvius Reigns

The master sat in the boat, his face turned to stone. No one said a word; only the rhythmic splashing of the oars dipping into water blended with the receding noise from the city. Pomponianus, watching from the bow, looked back towards Mount Vesuvius. A giant cloud, like an enormous treetop, had formed above the summit and spread rapidly. It changed from white to spotted grey, as if loaded with ash and earth. Again, flames licked from the crater and flashes of lightening lit the cloud. Milon was spellbound, facing the stern as he rowed, watching the uncanny sight of the mountain covered in smoke and vapour, spitting out fire. The cloud rolled nearer to Pompeii.

Suddenly, Fuscus, who sat at the helm, shouted, "Master, ash is falling into our boat. It could catch fire!"

Indeed, the flakes were falling like grey snow. They could be ground to flour in your hand. Suddenly, as if it was hailing, water sprayed up around the boat. Smaller pieces of stone rained down on them. They reached the bank on the other side of the river, landing next to a larger ship that also belonged to Pomponianus.

The master, his usual self-restraint and calm now lost in fear, ordered, "Quick, up to the villa! If the firestones start to fall hotter and bigger, my whole house will burn. Carry everything that can be saved down to the ship. We will sail out to sea!"

Up in the villa, the family and servants were confused. Pomponianus' wife rushed crying into his arms. She had feared for his life. But he repeated his orders and immediately, cases and boxes, food supplies, bundles of cloth and carpets were hurried down to the river and onto the ship. The carriers had to cover their heads from falling stones and warm ash.

Milon picked up one of the bigger pieces that landed in front of him, feeling the dying heat. Despite its size, it was strangely light and smelt like sulphur. This was no ordinary stone broken off a rock; it was slag from the fires of the underworld, the smithy of Hephaestus. But there was no time to contemplate. As he carried his load onto the ship he noticed a four-man rowing boat approaching. The passengers disembarked and hurried towards Pomponianus' ship.

A dignified older gentleman asked, "Is Pomponianus up there in his house?" Milon said yes and the stranger climbed the steps towards the villa with his attendants.

Setting his load down on the ship, Milon saw two guards dipping long brushes into water buckets to splash the planks of the ship, where hot ash and water formed a grey steaming pulp. Hurrying to the villa again, Milon kept his head covered with a leather apron to protect himself from the falling stones. He arrived at the top to see Pomponianus stepping out under the veranda to greet the unexpected visitor. They must have been old friends, for Pomponianus put his arms around him and cried out, "Plinius, it is you! The gods have sent you to me in this terrible hour."

The stranger, tall and imperious, smiled and gestured reassuringly with his hand. "Why have you all gone mad like this? If a mountain spits out a bit of ash and pumice, it doesn't mean the world will end! My friend, you don't want to sail down the Sarnus out to sea and then return after a few hours of sailing around lost, do you?"

Pomponianus was at a loss for words. The visitor continued, "Dear friend, I was going to sail upstream to the court of Cessus Bassus, but the hail of stones has driven me to you. Let's eat and drink and be at peace together until Vesuvius has calmed down again."

These words worked wonders. Pomponianus calmed down and ordered Fuscus to stop carrying things to the ship. Then he turned to his visitor. "Plinius, my friend, I thought you were in Rome. What brings you to this part of the world?"

"I'm stationed as commander of the imperial fleet over in

Misenum and I found time to visit old friends, to stop them from doing foolish things!"

With that they disappeared inside the house. Fuscus announced grandly, "This is one of the mightiest Romans. He rules over thousands and is afraid of nothing; even if the jaws of the earth broke open before him, he would show no fear."

As Fuscus said these words, the stones drummed down harder and the tiles on the roof began to break. At Fuscus' command, Milon went to the kitchen where, with Tyrios, he prepared the table for the distinguished guests.

The Fall

When the long meal ended, Milon went out to the veranda to watch the threatening mountain. Ash lay ankle deep over the gardens. It was already very dark, although it was only just after noon. An enormous fire-fountain flamed through the fog of smoke from Vesuvius.

After the meal, Pomponianus, his family and their guests came outside. Horrified, they exclaimed, "The whole mountain burns!"

But Plinius calmed them. "Those are just a few farmhouses on the slopes of the mountain burning. Let's take a rest for a while. The mountain will have had its fling. The rage of the gods is like the rage of humans: it doesn't last."

So they went back inside. Plinius lay down for a nap in a chamber that led off the courtyard. The rain of ash and stones continued.

About an hour later, a violent earthquake began. It seemed as if the walls of the buildings were sliding to the ground. There was a terrible crash and everyone ran out to the veranda to see what was happening. Someone woke Plinius; they had to force open the door from the courtyard, which was blocked with ash and stones. Plinius finally realised that the situation was getting worse, and if they stayed there the house may collapse, so he and Pomponianus considered where they could flee.

News came from the river Sarnus that no large boats could get through, as the shallows were filled with ash and stones. There was a strong head wind, which hindered access to the sea, even for smaller boats.

Suddenly a beam and some tiles fell from the roof. After a lot of panicked back and forth, in which only Plinius remained calm, they decided to flee to the fields to the southeast, as far as possible from the raging mountain.

"If the house falls we'll be buried alive!" cried Pomponianus. They tied pillows or clutched baskets to their heads as protection from the stone-rain. The slaves were ordered to bring food, drink and blankets. It was dark as night when the ghostly train left the villa, guided by wind-lights. When they passed the fishpond, in a distant flash of lightening, Milon caught sight of the dancing faun, still playing his flute in the ash. He seemed to be grinning at the terrified, fleeing humans.

Progress over the ash- and stone-covered field was difficult. Some slipped, fell and needed help to stand. Children cried and wailed, and screams of terror were heard between the constant clatter of stones. Everyone kept close together through fear of getting lost in the darkness. Fuscus, at Plinius' order, led the train south towards the sea, where they might be able to escape via the water. They moved more and more slowly as the dusty air made breathing harder.

Suddenly Plinius sank exhausted to the ground. Tyrios spread out a blanket for him. He asked for cold water, which was brought to him in a jug. He drank twice. Then the hot wind brought a smell of stinging sulphur, which forced them onwards. Leaning on Tyrios and Milon, Plinius stood up, then in the next moment he fell — dead — between them. Their horror and bewilderment was now complete. There was only one way forward, so the dead were left behind without guardians, near the shore, covered with a blanket.

As they carried on, the stone-rain decreased, but ash still fell like snow in winter. There was further alarm when the Pomponianus' wife fell, although supported by her husband and a slave. She lost her composure and screamed, "There are no gods in heaven! The last night is upon us, the eternal night which will swallow our earth!" She was made to rest on a heavy blanket, and four slaves carried the wretched woman onwards. Pomponianus and his two daughters walked beside her, trying to calm her.

Finally, between the ash clouds, they saw a glimmer of daylight low in the sky, where the late afternoon sun revealed grey dusty figures fleeing through a white, dead world. With the increasing light came a glimpse of hope, though the earth still rocked from time to time. Over the river, in the direction of Pompeii, everything was still shrouded in darkness. Distant thunder told them that the city, which they had seen flourishing that morning, was falling behind them.

Suddenly, in front of the fugitives arose the dark outlines of a ghostly orange tree with golden fruit still shining among the grey leaves, as if from an unreal past. A barn stood nearby; its firm posts had survived the earthquake.

Pomponianus stopped the train and ordered, "Here we stop. Make a camp for the masters and mistresses. Perhaps in the morning we may be able to return."

They began to clear the ash and stones away from entrance to the barn. Suddenly the low evening sun broke through the blanket of cloud over the sea and created an unreal, burning red landscape of ash, veiled in smoke. Tyrios climbed up into the orange tree and shook the branches. A thick cloud of dust rose up and some fruit fell. Swiftly he collected them in a basket, which he had carried over his head. He rubbed the skins with a towel and presented the rare fruit to his master, who seized them thankfully — an unexpected gift from the earth, which had turned to hell.

Tyrios always understands how to make himself popular with his master, Milon thought. Meanwhile he had prepared a bed of straw for the servants on the ashy ground. There was plenty of straw in the barn.

Suddenly Fuscus said, "Milon, you will be part of a group who will come with me this evening to Stabiae. Pomponianus doesn't want to leave the boat full of cargo unattended. Prepare yourself to go back. We will leave shortly."

How Milon would have liked to spread himself on the straw bed after all this effort!

But a little later Fuscus and six younger slaves walked towards the sea, hoping to find an easier way along the coast in the night. The dying sun sank into the water. Fuscus carried the only burning torch, whose glass shield protected the flame from the wind. Many dead fish lay on the beach, thrown from the waves onto stone cinders. Rocks had pushed back the water and filled large strips of the riverbed.

Tyrios had been kept to serve his master, so Milon missed his friend, who had always shared his joy and sadness. Silently the slaves marched, following the torch. The rain of stones and ash had stopped. Only now and then the wind drove clouds of choking dust before them. Overcame with exhaustion, Milon thought he might fall asleep and sink to the ground, but on they went. Once they met fugitives, who were using the coast as an escape route. Fuscus stopped some of them. They had terrible news.

"Pompeii is buried — over and over! The city is covered in a shroud of ashes. There are no living souls left. Thousands are buried among the ruins. Liquid fire flowed down in broad streams from Vesuvius into the city." The fugitives urgently warned Fuscus not to continue. "Back! Behind us lies only death and ruin!"

Fuscus asked about the river Sarnus, and one replied, "We left the city by crossing the river. It had been filled by the stone-rain. We had waited too long in our house, which stood close to the river. It was buried, but in the end we found a way out." Then he hurried on after the others.

Fuscus tried to encourage himself. "Less than an hour and we'll be at the boat. There we'll find shelter and a bed."

Who could describe the terror of Fuscus and the slaves as they approached the gardens and villa of Pomponianus. Stones and ash lay piled as high as a man. The wall of the house had collapsed on one side and the roof was completely ruined. Nothing could be seen of the faun and the fishpond. As they trudged towards the boat they saw just two wooden masts protruding from a huge pile of debris. A desolate hill of stone and ash had spread from the shore over the deck. From the other bank of the Sarnus, where the town lay, flames flickered from burnt-out buildings. Luckily wind blew the smoke in the other direction.

Fuscus and his helpers began to free a path to the ship, painfully slowly, lit by the meagre glow of the wind-light. It was nearly midnight before they could enter the stern of the boat through a hatch. The inside was completely unscathed and Pomponianus' things lay untouched in their places. The exhausted slaves lay down on carpets and sacks as Fuscus refilled the oil in the wind-light.

Milon didn't fall asleep as quickly as his companions. In his mind he relived the journey. He took the coin Alkides had given him on the Acropolis from his belt and pressed it to his forehead. He wanted to say thank you for saving him from the horror of the day, but his lips couldn't find the words. He felt as if the gods of Athens had not come with him. The Roman gods seemed to be enemies of the people; they allowed such horrors to happen. He whispered snatches of prayers from the sacrifices on the Acropolis, which he had sealed in his memory. And in his inner eye, he could just glimpse images of the temples. He put the coin carefully back in his belt pocket. Homeless in the Roman land, with the taste of bitter ash on his tongue, Milon fell asleep.

The Dead City

After yesterday's experience, Fuscus, who had often been feared by the slaves, became strangely quiet and more friendly. Normally he would have woken the sleeping slaves with a blow of his stick. Today he was content to push the dirty sole of his foot into the side of the one lying nearest to him and to rasp a comradely, "Up, up, you lads!"

From the provisions of the ship there was hard bread with dried fish for breakfast, and water from a barrel that had been filled only the day before. After that he commanded the slaves, "Your first task is to free the ship from stones and ash. It cannot sail any more. When Pomponianus returns today, he and his family will have to live in the boat. Only rats and mice could live up in the villa. Up! To work!"

There were enough tools, baskets and brooms on the boat, and soon they began shovelling and clearing the deck. Pumice and ash were thrown into the riverbed, so a wall of rocks grew around the boat. The volcanic rock was quick to clear because it was five times lighter than normal stone. By midday the whole deck was cleared and a small wall was raised as an access path. After a short meal, Fuscus granted them a midday rest. He himself drank a jug of wine slept.

Milon asked one of the other slaves named Vargo, "Would you come with me over the Sarnus to catch a glimpse of Pompeii? Fuscus will have a long sleep."

"Gladly, I'll come with you," Vargo replied.

Armed with sticks to help them walk, they crossed the riverbed. The water trickled sparsely, hidden under a high, porous stone layer that had filled the riverbed. When they had struggled up the rubble-covered bank on the other side, Milon cried out in horror. A smoking, grey stone desert stretched over the former city as far as the eye could see. There were no houses or living beings in sight. Vesuvius had grown mightily behind. A white plume of smoke rose from the summit far into the distance. Looking more closely, Milon noticed that the stone desert was uneven. There were long stone ditches where lanes and streets had been. Where large buildings had stood there were higher stone hills.

"Listen! I can hear a dog barking," said Vargo.

Yes, Milon too could hear an occasional muffled bark not far away.

"Is the poor fellow buried alive somewhere?" Vargo guessed.

"Come, let's search for him!"

Carefully, stumbling along a ditch, they could still feel warmth glowing through the stones and ash below. It was eerie, this walk through the town of the dead, which had yesterday been full of colourful life and bustle. They stopped suddenly as a small stone hill collapsed and smoke came shooting out. A roof had fallen in, the burnt beams no longer able to carry the mass of stone. The dog's barking sounded closer and louder and at a corner, when the stone ditch-path turned, they both saw him. He was digging and barking helplessly.

"He's looking for someone, dead or alive, perhaps his master is buried down there," said Vargo. The animal didn't run away when they arrived but continued to dig.

"I'll go and fetch shovels and be back soon!" called Milon. He returned with ropes, a jug of water and some bread. He threw a piece to the dog, which jumped on it hungrily.

"I examined the place with a stick," said Vargo, "and I got quite a few of the stones out of the way. It would take too long to reach the entrance as the stones slide down while you work. But I think we could free one corner of the roof, take away the tiles and try to climb inside."

Feverishly they started on the task. It was as if the animal understood that they wanted to help. His barking grew quieter. It didn't take long to throw the stones and ash from one corner of the house into the ditch. The roof tiles were easy to remove, and through the open beams they could look down into a large hall. Milon and Vargo put their heads through the opening.

Vargo called into the dark, "Is anyone down there?"

From the depths of a cellar came a weak, wailing response.

The dog tried to squeeze beside them into the small opening and started to bark again.

"There's someone alive down there!" Vargo exclaimed. "Milon, you're slender and light. I'll lower you down on a rope and pull you up again when you've found the survivor."

Vargo quickly knotted the rope to a roof beam and Milon lowered himself down. When he first felt the floor under his feet, he had to adapt his eyes to the darkness. The air smelt thick with sulphur. Vargo broke some more tiles to let in a little more light. When he could see more clearly, Milon shrank back. Motionless bodies lay there, suffocated by the sulphur fumes. Through a doorway hung and tied with a thick rug, Milon now heard the pitiful crying of a child. Amongst the dead there was still *one* living soul! He untied the wall rug and pulled it aside.

Into the dark space he said softly, "Where are you? Come to me!"

Suddenly the arms of a little boy embraced him. He was sobbing, his whole body quivering. Milon lifted him up and tried to comfort him. The boy, his eyes filled with tears, didn't recognise the bodies of his parents. He looked upwards to the daylight where the dog whimpered. Milon fastened the boy, who appeared to be about seven years old, onto his back with his belt and let strong Vargo pull them up.

Reaching down between the beams, feet on the wall, Vargo took the boy from Milon's back. The child covered his eyes with both hands at the painful dazzle of light, but the dog came to him immediately, whimpering joyfully and licking his arms and legs. Then the boy took one hand from his eyes and hugged the dog, calling him by his name, "Carus!"

Vargo said, "The dog probably ran out of the city at the start of the earthquake and came back to search for his people."

He reached out for the tiles and closed the opening again

while Milon offered the boy, who called himself Florus, a mug of water to drink. He savoured it thirstily, in long draughts, and gratefully took a piece of bread. As his eyes became accustomed to the daylight, his gaze wandered, numbed and horrified over the stone desert. He couldn't understand what had happened or where he was. He only remembered a terrible noise and then darkness. He must have been lying unconscious for a long time.

"We have to go back to Fuscus," said Vargo. "Milon, you carry the boy and I'll take the dog on the rope."

When they arrived back, they found that Fuscus had woken from his afternoon sleep and was furious at their absence. But seeing that they'd returned from Pompeii with the dog and boy, he didn't scold them. He recognised the boy's name as being from a well-known, noble family, and praised Vargo and Milon for their courage. The dog was tied to the deck. Florus followed Milon everywhere because he had freed him from the darkness, but he soon lay down in the hold of the ship on a blanket and fell into a deep sleep.

Vargo and Milon stayed on the ship to prepare for Pomponianus' return. Fuscus made his way up to the villa with the four other slaves to search through the rubble and ruins for anything they could salvage. In the late afternoon a messenger came to report that the master and his family were near. Vargo told Fuscus, who promptly returned to the ship with his helpers, carrying tools and sacks.

A tired procession dragged itself along as Pomponianus, his family and attendants approached the ship. Their bodies were bent with fear, hopelessness and exhaustion. Their distraught eyes peered about. Pomponianus brightened a little as he walked onto the ship, seeing the work they'd done there. His family sank exhausted onto the comfortable couches they had made from bales. Pomponianus couldn't praise Fuscus enough for how well he'd organised everything. At the front of the ship there was room for the master and his family; under the stern deck, were sleeping places for the servants and their children.

Later, on a tour through the ship, Fuscus led his master to the boy and his dog, who lay sleeping together in a corner under the stern deck. He told him of the wonderful rescue. When the boy awoke and was brought on deck, Pomponianus cried out, "Are you not Florus, the son of Attikus? Only yesterday I was your guest in Pompeii."

The boy nodded. Tears sprang to his eyes as he recognised his father's friend. Pomponianus was moved and took him into his arms to comfort him. He carried him to the master cabin, to his wife and two daughters. He described the discovery of the buried boy and ended by saying, "So, the downfall of Pompeii has given me a son and you a brother. He will stay with us now."

"And the dog too!" said Lulla, his youngest daughter. And so it was.

The Dancing Faun

Another day began. Pomponianus had spent a sleepless night considering the situation. He had visited his villa the evening before and realised that his property was completely destroyed. It wasn't possible to save anything and even if the house was still standing, he and his family could never stay in this place of horror again. They would never know when Vesuvius was going to wreak havoc again. Away from here! The sooner the better! Anyway, he owned a second villa in Rome, which was his main residence. He decided to move there as soon as possible. But before that he had to take care of Plinius, find his body and inform his relatives in Misenum of the disaster. Plinius' four companions, who had rowed him here, were sent to look for their dead master.

Fuscus and some of the slaves had been busy since the early hours trying to clear stones and ash from the rowing boat. When Pomponianus inspected it and found it undamaged, he had it carried along the bank of the Sarnus down to the sea, so they could sail it over to Misenum. There he would find a ship which would take them all to Rome.

The slaves carried the boat down to the river, and before he departed to Misenum, Pomponianus told Fuscus, "Tomorrow I'll return to Stabiae with the ship Plinius commanded in the imperial flotilla. It's a large ship, which will give the last honours to the dead and carry his body to Rome. They will need to anchor quite far from the shore. A smaller boat can carry the body to the ship, once it is found. My servants will take the most important goods to the ship. You can keep three slaves. Stay with them on the boat on the Sarnus. Save anything of value from the ruins of the villa that can be brought to Rome later."

With this Pomponianus left and Tyrios was one of the four

rowers assigned to go with him. Misenum was on the opposite side of the Bay of Naples, which the Romans called Sinus Puteolanus, so it would be a day's journey.

Towards evening, one of the four who had been sent to find Plinius returned to tell Fuscus, "After a lot of searching, we found Plinius' body, totally unspoilt and so are his robes. He lay there as if he was asleep. We carried him to a shelter, close to the sea. The three others are keeping the death-watch until the ship arrives."

The messenger asked Fuscus for two oil lamps, so they wouldn't have to spend the whole night in darkness with the dead. He was given food and drink for his companions and promised to come back in the morning to report the arrival of the ship.

Next day, around noon, a proud ship of the imperial flotilla anchored between Stabiae and Pompeii. Boats were lowered and Pomponianus came ashore. Plinius' body was carried to the ship. As a friend of Caesar's, a funeral pyre would be arranged for him, with great pomp. Pomponianus saw that his own cargo was loaded, and his family and most of his servants went on board.

Before leaving he said to Fuscus, "Don't forget to dig out the fawn near the fishpond. I'd like to set him up in my garden in Rome. One of my merchant vessels will arrive in about two weeks to collect the rest of my things. The ship in the Sarnus cannot be saved, unless Caesar were to send an army of soldiers to clear out the riverbed and make it navigable again. And another thing: when my goods have been collected, sell the three slaves that I'm leaving here to the highest bidder in Misenum. I won't need them in my household in Rome."

Fuscus promised to take care of everything to the master's satisfaction. Among the three chosen by Fuscus as helpers were Milon and Vargo. Tyrios, who had returned from Misenum with Pomponianus, came quickly to Milon. "I've heard that you're staying for now. I could beg Pomponianus to let you come with us to Rome, if you like?"

"Thanks, Tyrios, but I'm in no hurry to get to Rome. Whether it's two weeks earlier or later doesn't matter to me. Let's not bother our master with requests too soon. One day there may be something more important to ask for."And so it remained.

"See you in Rome!" Tyrios called to him in farewell; then their paths parted. They didn't know what Pomponianus and Fuscus had agreed, about the sale of the three slaves.

Fuscus and his slaves watched the departing boat. Milon remembered how Agaya had waved after him in Piraeus. Watching his friend sail away, he felt a painful loneliness and sadness creep over him; for little Florus, too, who had become dear to him, and who always wanted to ride on his shoulder again, as he'd done when he was carried through the dead city. They both sailed away on the proud ship.

Walking back along the stone-filled Sarnus, Fuscus told them what their work would be. In fourteen days everything usable must be salvaged from the ruins and stowed on the ship, ready to be taken to Rome. But he said nothing of what was to happen to them. Milon was glad that Vargo had stayed too, for they had got on well since finding Florus together.

The days passed slowly until the excavation of the Faun, which Milon, Vargo and the third slave, Vesonius, dug out of the ash and stone. Fuscus himself had to help carry the heavy dancer down to the ship. As he stood on the foredeck, Milon noticed that the faun was facing towards Pompeii and Vesuvius, and it seemed as if he was playing a mocking song on his flute about the vain struggles and strivings of humankind. Suddenly, Milon had an uncanny thought: *In Rome's gardens, the faun might witness the fall of that imperial city too, and play a song of flowering and fading, of dying and eternity on his Greek flute.* It was almost as if he felt a kinship with the dancing faun, who through everything that happened around him, played his music and remained serene.

New Destinations

Three weeks went by before a small vessel from Pomponianus arrived. With the help of the crew, the cargo was transferred out of the ship in the Sarnus. Less could be saved from the ruined villa than they had expected. The captain reminded Fuscus that they would stop at Misenum to sell the three slaves. But if they couldn't get a good price, they should be brought back to Rome.

It was only on the voyage over the Sinus Puteolanus that Fuscus told them, "I have orders to sell you in Misenum. The master doesn't need you in Rome."

Vargo and Vesonius remained calm, but Milon turned pale. *Never again to see his friend Tyrios? Never again to carry little Florus on his shoulder?* Milon felt that destiny had intervened. He remembered how he himself had chosen to stay in Stabiae when Tyrios had offered to ask for them to stay together.

Milon looked across the sea towards the cloud-laced beauty of Vesuvius, rising out of the blue waters. There must be a fiery path into the inner earth at its peak. His thoughts weighed heavily. *Have the gods sent this destruction as punishment for crimes which have never been atoned for? But then too many innocents have suffered. Or is humanity like one great body, in which guilt and atonement are brought to balance?*

Milon found no answer to his questions. He saw the coast of Misenum approaching and the ship came to life. Fuscus brought a chain and fastened the three slaves. Almost with an apology, he explained, "I trust you not to run away, but it's the custom during the sale."

Never before had Milon worn chains. The cold iron pressing into his wrists reminded him that, at this moment, he was not classed as a human being. Like the rope-bound bales from the ship, he was just classed as goods.

When the ship was moored in the harbour, with many proud Roman ships alongside, Fuscus ordered, "Stay on the ship until I have dealt with my business."Not an hour had passed, when he returned with an interested dealer. Then they were examined thoroughly and Fuscus went aside to haggle about the price until they came to an agreement.

Before leaving the ship, Fuscus thumped Milon and Vargo on the shoulder. "Good fellows, don't be afraid," he said. "You won't end up on a war galley; you are too good for that. Your new master travels over the sea to Africa, to the city of Alexandria. You will have another long voyage. Have a good journey!"

Without touching the shore of Misenum they were taken to a medium sized sailing vessel, bearing the name *Alexandria*. Instead of hand chains, they now had a small ankle chain, from which they were only freed when the ship was on the high seas; slaves had been known to escape in the harbour before by swimming.

During this first night Milon hardly closed his eyes. The iron on his ankle clanked as he lay on his plank bed. Humiliation and uncertainty plunged him into a mood of desperation. In the middle of the night he took the coin of Alkides from his belt. It had comforted him before. In the darkness he put the coin between his teeth and bit on it hard to fight his rising tears. He thought of Athens, but every time he tried to envisage the temple of the Acropolis, the dancing faun appeared, and the smoke-clouds of Vesuvius enveloped its fair, shining pillars. It was as if two worlds wrestled with each other. He turned over, frustrated, the clank of chains extinguishing his memories.

The journey took several weeks with good and mild winds until, out of the haze, a high tower arose, which the ship's crew greeted as the lighthouse of Alexandria, the signpost for Egypt. The land and its cities at the mouth of the Nile were, like Greece, under the rule of the Roman she-wolf, so Milon wasn't surprised to see many Roman ships and soldiers in the harbour. Not long after their arrival, in the early morning, the dealer asked the three slaves from Misenum to get washed and ready to go into town.

Vargo said to Milon, "That means the slave market for us. We will be sold!"

But Milon wasn't as apprehensive about setting foot on Egyptian soil as he had been in Roman lands, and he thought, *Perhaps the good star of Aphrodite has brought me to this land of Egypt.*

The Golden Titus

The trader, Calpurnicus, who owned the ship, approached the three slaves. "As you're such nimble and clever fellows," he said, "I've decided to keep you. I'll take three older ones to the market instead. They're not so quick at climbing or performing the ship's other duties. Soon we'll be loading grain to take to the beautiful town of Leptis Magna. Now, go and help unload the goods we've brought from Misenum!"

Soon after, Calpurnicus left the vessel with the three older slaves. Vargo said to Milon and Vesonius, "I like life on board a ship, especially when we stay together. We know how to eke out an existence here. I'm never sure what to expect with a new master. Let's try and stick together as good friends!"

"Yes, slaves need good friends," said Milon. "I welcome crossing the seas with you and seeing a bit of the world."

"To work!" called Vesonius. "We'll answer the decision of our master with good work. The bundles to be unloaded are over there." And with that, the three of them started work.

As Milon carried a bale on his back, to set foot on Egyptian soil for the first time, he jumped off the plank to greet the new land with both feet. But the weight on his back gathered momentum and he fell flat on his belly, the bundle rolling over his head. Behind him there was loud laugh. "Milon, you've greeted Egypt on your belly and your forehead! If I was a prophet I would foretell that a terrible fate awaits you in this land," said Vargo.

Rather ashamed, Milon stood up, but apart from a bump on his head he was unharmed. He quickly picked up the bale and said, "The Egyptian soil draws me; perhaps it would like to keep me!" and he laughed with Vargo, who often called him "Frog" from then on.

When Calpurnicus came back on his own at the end of day, Vargo said to Milon, "He sold them! He looks content and full to the neck with Egyptian wine. Look, he sways like a boat on the waves."

Calpurnicus had difficulty climbing on board. At the top of the footbridge, when he put his foot on the deck, he staggered and fell over a pile of rope. From a distance Vargo giggled, "Look, Milon, there's a second frog, soon he will croak!"

Calpurnicus began to curse about the thick rope and about the swaying of the ship, which lay unmoving in the water. Then he noticed that some silver coins had fallen from his bag and he shouted, "My money! My beautiful money! Bring my money back!"

Some of the coins had already rolled overboard, where the footbridge joined the deck, and had plummeted into the water between the ship's side and the harbour wall. Quickly the slaves searched for the scattered coins and gave them to the supervisor who had come running up.

"Everything given to me?" he asked sharply, looking round with suspicion. Everybody said yes.

The supervisor gave Calpurnicus a handful of silver coins. "Here's what we found. Any that rolled into the water will be lost in the mud."

"Oh, my beautiful money!" groaned Calpurnicus. "I must count it. All the silver Caesar coins and some new golden Titus-head coins. Beautiful new Titus-head coins!"

The supervisor ordered, "Vargo, Vesonius, help the master to his bunk. You others, disappear!" He guided his master inside the ship, to help count and put away the money.

A little later, when Milon was rolling a rope, he heard a clink of metal. A golden coin! He picked it up, and noticed an image on the coin. According to the inscription it was the broad head of Titus, who had become Caesar that year. Pomponianus and Plinius had spoken of him as their friend. Quickly, Milon glanced around. Nobody had noticed his find. He put the Titus into his belt with the Greek coin of Athena. Should he keep it?

From his bunk Vargo reported, "Calpurnicus was so drunk he couldn't even count his money. He couldn't tell the supervisor how much he'd received for the three slaves either."

The next day, the slaves had heavy labour. There were hundreds of sacks of grain to be fetched and loaded into the ship. When the day's work was done, Vesonius said, "As a boy, I used to dive for mussels on the coast. I'll try to find the silver coins under our ship!" He dived many times and dug into the thick mud, but no coins came up.

Milon wasn't sure what to do with the golden Titus coin. But when he thought of all his hard work, without payment, he decided to keep his find. You never know, in an hour of need, a Titus coin might save him.

To Leptis Magna and Portus Augusti

Heavily loaded with sacks of grain, the *Alexandra* sailed westward along the coast of North Africa. They landed at some of the harbours occupied by the Romans to fill up with fresh water and buy food. The journey took several weeks until they reached the splendid city of Leptis Magna. There were many pleasant hours of leisure during the voyage on the *Alexandra*. But on the days of loading and unloading, the work was heavy. Milon learnt that Calpurnicus was a grain dealer, who transported almost exclusively grain. Only on the return journey to Egypt would he carry a few other goods, occasionally even some passengers.

Much as Milon would have liked to go ashore, slaves didn't get the chance, except for loading and unloading at the port. After a long return journey to Alexandria, they had to load and unload once more, and when that was done, the monotonous life on sea, month after month and year after year, followed.

One day, while the ship was anchored at the port of Alexandria, Calpurnicus received a message that, from now on, the *Alexandra* would carry goods to Portus Augusti, near Rome. The supervisor explained, "Your master Calpurnicus will stay in Alexandria and I will be your master on the ship."

"Calpurnicus must be rich enough," Vargo whispered to Milon. "We've carried so many thousands of sacks for him."

The supervisor continued, "He's assigned a steward who will sail with us and share my command. We'll sail to the sea port of Rome, which is called Portus Augusti. Rome itself lies inland and can only be reached by a long road from the sea."

Milon got excited, hearing him talk of Rome, and Vargo asked, "Do you think we could look for Tyrios? Little Florus will have grown a lot by now!"

How would we find him in the largest city in the world! thought
Milon, but he was so excited his throat pounded. At last there
was new hope of more varied days in their tedious life.

Some weeks later they arrived at Portus Augusti, four hours
walk from Rome. The grain sacks were unloaded, and piled up
as high as a house under a tiled roof; from there they would be
carted by wagon to the city. As evening approached the carriers
worked slower and slower in the gathering dusk before all the
sacks were piled in place. Dead tired after their hard work, the

slaves sank down on the deck, gulping bitter barley drink from jugs.

Then the supervisor came over. "A day of rest tomorrow. You can recover your strength. The next day we'll load again and return to Alexandria. Our ship will stay anchored. No slave is allowed to leave!"

Vargo looked at Milon when he heard that, sensing his disappointment; he had hoped so much to go to Rome, and maybe see Tyrios and Florus again. Vargo moved closer to him and whispered, "Milon, surely the supervisor will go out this evening and stay in Rome all day tomorrow enjoying himself. I'll help you go secretly to the city."

"That's impossible! How could I get away without being noticed? The steward will stay on board when the supervisor goes."

"Yes, but surely one of us will have to run an errand ashore. I heard that we have to get water to fill up our barrels. I'll offer the two of us and Vesonius for that, then we'll let you sneak off to Rome. If someone asks for you, we'll say you're at the well. I'm sure you can catch a ride on one of the wagons that go to Rome all the time, and in the evening you'll be back."

With this, Vargo went up to the supervisor and offered himself and the two others as water carriers for the next day. "Master, we're the youngest, and we like to row the boat ashore to pass the time."

"All right, I'm sure you'll find a well. Fill all the barrels on the ship; Rome has better water than Alexandria."

As Vargo had guessed, only a short time later the supervisor was rowed ashore in the small boat, which was lowered, from the ship, and which they'd use the next day to fetch water.

Early the next morning, they found a well on the shore. Vargo urged Milon, "Go now, immediately, to the main street, the Via Portuensis; you'll find a vehicle there heading for Rome. In the evening when dusk falls, I'll wait for you here by the well. You'll have enough time in Rome to look for Tyrios."

"I will!" Milon exclaimed. "I'll ask for the house of the rich and famous Pomponianus. If I find the master, I'll also find his servant."

Despite the hope of possibly meeting Tyrios and Florus in Rome, Milon didn't feel comfortable in his skin. "Vargo, Vesonius! You're good friends, but what happens if I'm unlucky and the supervisor returns before me?"

Then we'll say you went to rest on the corn sacks under the tiled roof after collecting water, and you overslept. You could actually do that if you're late back. So then — good journey to Rome!"

Milon was lucky. Just then a carter came to the well with his leather kettle to water his two horses before driving up to Rome. Milon offered to water the animals for him, and the carter was pleased to accept. Soon they were driving together along the Via Portuensis to the city. They made good speed because the wagon was carrying fish, which had to arrive fresh for the morning market.

Meeting Again in Rome

The horses trotted along the cobbled Via Portuensis in the fresh morning air. Milon was amazed at the breadth of the road and how busy the traffic was so early in the morning.

"Why are you going to Rome?" asked the carter, who sat next to him on the bench.

"To visit a friend. He serves the noble Pomponianus."

"Ah, Pomponianus! Is he the owner of many ships, which trade here from Portus Augusti — a rich man?"

"Yes, that's him. Can you tell me how I can find his house in this giant city? I've never been to Rome."

"When we arrive at the market place, I'll direct you to the Capitoline Hill; his villa stands at the foot of that hill. Any street sweeper can show you the way."

Later that morning, as they drove into the city built on hills, with its temples and palaces, Milon was amazed at its size and the swarms of people. The shouting in the streets and noisy rattle of wheels were louder than he'd ever heard in Athens.

At the market place he bid farewell to the carter, who showed him the way. "There on the hill is the Capitol, a fortress with many temples. Head that way and you'll find the villa of Pomponianus."

Soon Milon stood before the open entrance gate to a park, where a stone tablet read: POMPONIANUS. As he stood deciding whether or not to go in, he heard footsteps approaching from inside. He moved aside as a tall, elegantly dressed youth came out accompanied by a slave.

That could be Florus! he thought, but he didn't dare to step in front of the elegant Roman. Everything seemed so strangely foreign to him. What was he doing here? He was about to leave when a fruit seller with a basket approached the gate.

Milon asked him, "Do you know if there's a slave called Tyrios in this house of Pomponianus?"

"Yes," replied the salesman, "he's a good customer of mine. You mustn't call him a slave though; not long ago he became his master's young housekeeper and now he commands the slaves. He does all the shopping too. I'm bringing this fruit for him. He's a capable fellow, and he's usually at home at this time. Come in with me if you want to speak to him."

At this the fruit seller entered and Milon followed. The man knocked at a small side door of the palatial villa, while Milon waited to one side. First a slave appeared then quickly disappeared, and Tyrios stepped out in splendid clothing. He checked the fruit quickly, and said, "Good, carry it to the kitchen."

The fruit seller pointed to Milon, who Tyrios hadn't noticed. "There is someone else who wants to speak to you."

Tyrios' eyes fell on the stranger, then he cried, "Milon! Is it you?" and immediately they were in each other's arms.

"By Jupiter, where have you come from? Are you well? Have you been in Rome long? Come, tell me! Let's sit in the garden by the fishpond. You know him, the dancing faun? He still blows his old flute, but unfortunately he came here without you."

The two old friends sat on the steps by the pond at the feet of the faun. How wretched Milon felt next to the fine Tyrios, who looked at him with pity. Milon struggled to find words. "Tyrios, I've hardly been in Rome an hour and I can't stay long. I drove secretly from Portus Augusti early this morning to find you. This evening I must be back at the ship to which I was sold after the fall of Pompeii. All these years I've been serving on the ship, bringing Egyptian grain to harbours of the Roman Empire."

"So, is this the first time you've seen Rome, Milon? It's a wonderful city, with circus games, chariot races and exciting festivals. Our young Florus has already become a daring charioteer. He just left to train his horses as there's a big race in a few days. You should see it, Milon. That's no life for you, carrying corn sacks year after year. Pomponianus could buy you back! But he's away for a few days. As you can see, I've come to honour and now I'm responsible for all the housekeeping. Wouldn't you like to come back to us?"

Milon watched the goldfish playing in the water. "Tyrios, you may mock me, but sailing on the sea, sharing joy and suffering with my comrades in days of hard work, depresses me less than what I've seen of this crowded city. Maybe one day we'll sail to Greece and I can see Athens again."

"Are you still clinging to your dreams of the gods? In Rome I've learnt that only earthly matters count. I've managed to save a lot of money. Pomponianus is growing old. When he dies one day, I'll buy myself free from his heirs. Maybe I'll even succeed before that. One must always be striving for a goal, Milon. I've reached one goal: I'm indispensable to my master; the house and servants are firmly under my control."

Tyrios raised his head proudly, leaning back on one knee of the faun. Milon admired his self-assurance. Yes, he'd always been quite different from Tyrios, and yet he didn't envy the coloured ribbons shimmering with gold threads that were sewn onto his robes.

"Come!" said Tyrios. "You're invited to our meal! The master and mistress are away, so I can play the master."

He stood up, patted the back of the faun and took Milon into the house. Before the meal, he took his guest to his chamber and gave him clothing worthy of the table.

Milon could hardly believe his eyes as Tyrios led him to the great table of the house, where they lounged, couched on cushions for the meal. A servant and a slave girl carried in the dishes, as if they were masters of the house.

"I always eat with the masters, and when I'm alone, I let myself be served. Pomponianus taught me that one must keep a distance from the servants, if one wants to command them," said Tyrios, laughing, while he offered Milon a goblet of dark red wine.

"To good days in Rome! Tomorrow I'll drive to Portus Augusti with Florus and buy you for Pomponianus. You could serve here as Florus' stableboy, for his chariots and horses."

"This is strong wine the Romans drink," said Milon, as if he hadn't heard Tyrios' suggestion. "If I drank more than one goblet, I wouldn't be able to walk back!"

Tyrios laughed. "You fool! You don't have to go back on foot. Wearing these clothes, you can ride in one of the Roman citizens' chariots; they go regularly from the city to the sea and back. Have you money for the fare or shall I give you some?"

"I have money," answered Milon, who didn't intend to take any of the money that Tyrios had saved to buy his freedom. He was carrying the golden Titus in his girdle. What was more, a certain disappointment had crept over him during their meeting. It was as if the youthful friendship they'd shared had been swept away. Tyrios had become a clever, calculating Roman, while Milon was still an Athenian at heart.

The Journey Back

In the late afternoon, as Milon approached the city gate on the Via Portuensis, he saw some horse-drawn carriages through the crowds, waiting to take travellers towards the sea. He couldn't reach Portus Augusti in time on foot. Looking splendid in Tyrios' clothes, he went up to a chariot, drawn by two horses and asked, "Coachman, will you drive me to Portus Augusti?"

"Yes, noble sir, please climb in."

He stared, speechless, for a moment. "Noble sir," the coachman had said.

"Ah, the gentleman wants to know the fare? For a chariot and pair to Portus Augusti, one half Titus."

The coachman had expected the young gentleman to barter the price down, but that didn't happen. So with one jump he was on the carriage bench, calling, "Drive on!"

"The cushion, the cushion, noble sir!" cried the coachman, and he pushed a thick leather cushion towards Milon. Under one arm Milon firmly clasped the bundle of slave clothes; with the other hand he held on tight as the chariot moved off.

"Does the noble master wish to travel fast or slow?"

"Travel fast," Milon commanded. As the vehicle clattered under the arch of the gate, Milon turned to glance up at the city on the hill. Suddenly he thrust his hand into his girdle. Was the golden Titus actually still there? Yes, he could feel the hard circle encased in leather. It was there!

The wheels resounded on the cobbled street; sparks flew from the horses' hooves; a fresh breeze blew from the sea over Milon's face. He felt like the prince in a fairy tale. Once he laughed out loud, so the coachman turned and grinned cheerfully. Could life be so free and beautiful, with money? Two smart Roman women waved to him cheerfully from an approaching carriage, and he waved in reply and turned to look back at them, their bright scarves still fluttering in the wind.

"Portus Augusti!" cried the coachman after the long journey as he stopped by the harbour. With one spring from the chariot, Milon stood beside him and handed him the golden Titus.

"I need to find change," said the coachman, "I'll be back soon!"

"No need," replied Milon, "keep it all!"

The coachman had never received such a tip. Speechless, he stared at the "noble sir" to see if he was joking. When Milon lifted his hand in farewell, the coachman bowed before him, stammering, "Noble, magnanimous master, good master, best master ..." But Milon was already marching towards the harbour.

He searched for the well by the grain store, where Vargo should be waiting. He found him sitting on a stone bench, watching the colourful life of the harbour. Milon crept up from behind and struck him with one hand on the shoulder.

Startled, Vargo sprang up to see a nobly clad gentleman, who he assumed wanted to sit on the bench and drive him, the slave, away. He quickly stepped away.

Milon said cheerfully, "Don't you know me, Vargo? Clothes make the man!" He laughed in amusement at the face of his baffled friend, who clearly found it difficult to connect Milon's face with this noble exterior.

"Milon! You look like a nobleman! What's happened to you? Are you free? Aren't you coming back to our ship?"

"No, Vargo, look; here under my arm, I'm carrying the other ragged Milon. That's the one I'll put on again. It was beautiful to be master for a few hours, to ride in a chariot and wave at pretty Roman women."

He told Vargo about his adventures, then, before climbing into the rowing boat, Milon changed his clothes and the "noble master" was bound into a bundle with the same leather cord in which the "slave" had been rolled. Soon strong beats of the oars brought them back to the corn ship.

Next day, bales and casks had to be loaded and rowed out to

the anchored ship. Milon was one of the rowers. Each time they came ashore to load, he looked about, but Tyrios was nowhere to be seen, and Florus was surely too busy with his racehorses. As it was beginning to get dark, Milon pushed off from the shore for the last time. Then he knew that his way led back to Africa.

In the Storm

For a week the *Alexandra* fared, with a small freight, on course for Egypt. Then a gale swept up. Sails were quickly reefed in. Vesonius, rolling in the last sail with Vargo, cried, "Hold on to a rope, or the waves will carry us off into the sea like mice!"

A huge wave surged over the deck and caught Vargo, bringing him down. He was half overboard as the ship heeled.

Milon, emerging from below, where he had stowed the sailcloth, saw Vargo clinging dizzily to the edge of the ship. "Hold on, Vargo, I'll catch you!"

Despite the crashing waves, Milon and Vesonius managed to get a rope around Vargo, where he clung to the edge. They carried him, half unconscious, down into the ship.

Milon climbed the mast to bring in the last sail, which fluttered in the wind like a torn flag. Never before had he seen the sea so furious. He clung at the top of the wildly rocking mast for a moment, looking down at the raging water. Rain soaked his clothes; lightening flashed and thunder rolled above the roar of the waves.

Vesonius, who was waiting below for Milon, gasped as he saw him climb out onto a spar, trying to bring in the fluttering sail with one hand. Rain had hardened the knots and Milon struggled to loosen them, clenching his teeth. With part of the sail tucked under his arm, he worked on the last knot. Suddenly a gust of wind whipped at the sail and Vesonius saw a bright streak vanish into the storm. The sail was gone. Milon descended empty handed.

As they both dived below deck, Vesonius quoted, "A ship that loses a sail soon goes under, the old sailors say."

In the gloom below, the ship's crew cowered together fearfully, still hoping the storm would calm. Every joint of the ship creaked; nobody spoke a word. The supervisor and steward sat beside the slaves, all together in life or death, in the same peril and fear.

Suddenly a voice called out, "There's water in the hold!" They all leapt up. The lower hold was already knee-deep in water.

"Buckets here! Bail out! Form a chain up to the deck!"

After some confusion, a continual chain of leather buckets was passed from below, up a ladder and across the deck, to return again empty. The supervisor and steward went below to search for the leak, while the slaves feverishly bailed with buckets. In the faint glimmer of a wind-light, they saw that the stored corn was already deep in water. It was impossible to find the leak in the ship's hull. Despite bailing, the water remained knee-high.

Outside the huge waves continued to surge. For hours the water bailers worked, drenched in sweat. With dusk the wind subsided slightly, but the waves still threw the groaning ship relentlessly to and fro. Despite the bailing, the water had risen a hand's breadth higher. It was clear to everyone that the hidden crack in the hull of the ship was getting wider. The supervisor ordered them to take turns in two teams to bail.

Milon and Vargo were in the first group, who were now lying down in the centre of the ship's hull, completely exhausted, drinking water and chewing some hard bread.

"We're about three days away from Alexandria, time enough to sink," said Milon.

"With this crazy bailing, we could hold out for three days, but this old chest might suddenly break apart," said Vargo.

When they returned to work, Milon noticed that the seawater had risen. Their exhausted comrades rushed to the water jugs to wet their dry tongues and then collapsed to the ground as if they were dead. With the refreshed team, the buckets went at twice the speed; it seemed as if the waters were sinking a little. But they couldn't keep up this pace for long, and as the buckets slowed the water rose again. So it went, taking turns through the night.

At dawn the wind had almost dropped. The sails could be raised. The sea grew calmer. But inside the ship, water had reached the centre of the hull, which was both living and bedroom for them all. Although the ship had little freight, it slumped alarmingly deep in the water and sailed sluggishly. The water bailing grew more and more frantic because now it was a matter of life and death to survive the floods. The one small rowing boat onboard was just big enough to save the supervisor and the steward with two rowers.

The steward gave an order to get ready to wave cloths to call for help if a ship was sighted. There were only a few jugs of fresh water left and the slaves were terribly thirsty.

In one of his rest hours, Milon climbed up the mast and searched the wide surface of the sea. "Vesonius!" he called down suddenly. "I think I see a sail in the distance!"

Vesonius climbed quickly up to Milon's side. The whitish gleam was faint, but clear enough, and Vesonius confirmed, "Yes, it's a ship. It's heading in almost the same direction as we are. If we steer slightly to the east, we'll be near it."

Milon called down, "Quick! Tell the helmsman! I'll stay up here and point out the direction. It's still far behind us, but it seems to be on course for Alexandria."

At the call "A ship!" all the crew, with or without buckets, hurried on deck and peered into the distance where Milon was pointing.

Suddenly the supervisor thundered, "Do you all want to drown? Get bailing! Gaping around won't save us!"

Quickly the bailing began again, now full of hope and renewed strength. The upper cabin was already knee-deep in water. There was no dry place inside the ship now to lie down.

The helmsman set course, aiming to intercept the faster ship. Milon stayed above as pilot. Vesonius was the messenger between them.

"Course good!" Milon called down after a while. "I can already see the different sails."

Meanwhile, the supervisor and Vesonius had tied a cloth to a long pole, which they waved back and forth, signalling distress. The steward allowed the thirsty slaves the last drink of water from the jugs. Now they could see the other ship's sail from the deck. There were suppressed cries of joy.

How people cling to life, thought Milon, from up on his high post. *Even the most wretched slaves love it.*

"Milon!" shouted Vargo from below. "Here's the last drink for you. There's not another drop left in the jugs and barrels."

Milon climbed swiftly down. He had a burning thirst, and he drank the last of the water in deep gulps.

"Thanks, Vargo! I almost tumbled down from exhaustion and dizziness. I'll go back to bailing. The ship won't escape us now."

"Milon!" called the supervisor. "Come and wave the flag with Vesonius!"

Soon the flag wavers shouted, "They're answering! They've understood!" Cloths were waving from the other ship too now. All the water bailers hurried on deck again to see it with their own eyes, but the supervisor soon chased them back to work.

As they grew close, the crew on the other ship began to understand what was happening. They shouted that they would try to come alongside. All sails on the *Alexandra* were lowered, and she hung like a raft in the water.

"Bring everything that can be saved on deck," said the supervisor. So the bailing ceased; sails, ropes, barrels, jugs and the last provisions were piled together. The sea was calm, but the lower deck was now waist-deep in water.

Grappling hooks were thrown across to the *Alexandra* and the crowd cheered. The first to cross to the sailing vessel were the steward and supervisor, who greeted and embraced the Roman captain of the *Neptunus*. Then wooden planks were laid from ship to ship for the slaves to carry the cargo. Eventually everyone was on board the *Neptunus*, including the rowing boat, and the planks were pulled away. They loosened the grappling hooks, and the *Alexandra* sank slowly into the water.

Milon stood with Vargo on the rear deck of the *Neptunus*. "We couldn't have stayed above water half a day longer," said Vargo. "I'd made an escape plan for us three. One of the empty barrels we carried over is knotted into a fishing net, and we could have tied our belts to it."

"It was a good idea, Vargo, but your barrel would only have prolonged our torment if we'd not been discovered soon. Who notices a floating barrel in the vast ocean?"

"You're right, but every drowning man clings to a plank. What would our lives be without hope?"

"A slave lives on the hope that, once in a hundred horrible days, a better one will come. But now, until Alexandria, Vargo, our hours are carefree."

It was a good time. Three days calm journey, without work or worry and with enough food and drink. As the well-known coast came in sight, the supervisor gathered the slaves of the *Alexandra* together.

"Before we go ashore, you should know that the sinking of the *Alexandra* will be a great loss for our master Calpurnicus. He may not buy another ship. The captain of the *Neptunus* has agreed that we may stay a few days as his guests. Our steward will consult with Calpurnicus to decide what's going to happen to you. You'll stay here with me to help unload until the decision is made."

With these words he left the slaves alone. Vargo turned to Milon. "I'm sure Calpurnicus won't buy a new ship. We'll be sold. The market in Alexandria is the best place for that."

Vargo's suspicion was confirmed. After two days, the whole crew of the *Alexandra* was taken to the slave market in the great city.

A New Master

Although Milon had changed masters, he'd never been displayed in a public slave market before. Vargo had advised him to put on the Roman robe from Tyrios that he'd saved from the *Alexandra*.

"You look magnificent in this; surely you'll be bought into a high-ranking household and you can avoid the galleys!"

"I've had enough of sailing for a good while," Milon agreed. " I'd rather serve on land."

The slaves of the *Alexandra* were shown in the market with hundreds of others. Milon wanted to stay with Vargo as they'd become good friends. "How will we manage not to get separated, Vargo? You always come up with good ideas."

But Vargo was subdued and sad. All he could say was, "This time I have no idea."

The ship's owner, Calpurnicus, also came to the market, to agree good prices for his slaves and so ease the loss of his boat. The buyers came and went.

An elderly, rich Egyptian woman, in colourful dress, came with her housekeeper. "What's the price of this one?" she asked, pointing to Milon. Calpurnicus told her a sum that made her shriek. "I could buy *two* others for that much money! By evening, he'll be cheaper. We'll come back later."

Vargo said scornfully, "I hope that old nanny goat doesn't buy you. You'd have to bleat to her every call!"

"You're right! I'd rather be on a ship or tending real goats."

A sailor, who Calpurnicus knew, stood aside with him for a long time bargaining. He eventually bought Vargo, Vesonius and two others for his ship.

Milon summoned up all his courage to approach Calpurnicus and asked, "Would it be possible for me to stay together with Vargo and Vesonius?"

Calpurnicus looked at him with surprise. "You're too valuable for ship service. I'm selling you for a princely sum!"

Milon would have loved to tear off his rich clothing; he thought Tyrios' robe was the reason he was being separated from his friends. He cursed the idea that had led to him wearing it. With tears in his eyes he embraced Vargo and said goodbye; this friend with whom he'd rescued the child from the ruins of Pompeii, and for which they'd received so little thanks.

"Goodbye, Vargo! We'll not forget each other!"

Vargo nodded dumbly. He couldn't find any words. Then Milon saw the four slaves disappear into the crowded market.

It was nearly midday when a stern Roman, accompanied by a slave, stopped to examine him thoroughly.

"Have you served in a noble house before?" he asked.

"Twice, master!"

"Where?"

"Once in Greece, in the house of Midias in Athens."

"And the other time?"

"In Stabiae, in the house of Pomponianus."

"The rich and famous ship owner? Why did he not keep you?"

"Master, after the fall of Pompeii the house and estate in Stabiae were destroyed, and he dissolved his household."

"So you were present during those terrible days?"

"Yes, master, I saw the fall of that once thriving city."

The Roman turned again to Calpurnicus, and they agreed the deal.

A short time later, Milon sat with another slave called Lesco in a wagon. The Roman who had bought them sat next to the driver. Soon the wagon rumbled out of the city, heading south. Later they turned west and drove fast for many hours in the heat, with only short breaks at drinking wells. Milon sat quietly and sadly, while Lesco tried to make conversation.

"The man who bought us isn't the master. He's the steward. I overheard it at the market. I hope it'll be a clean service! I came from an elegant house in Alexandria, where there was little work, and we ate like the master. Where have you been?"

"On a boat carrying sacks of grain."

"Ah … and your beautiful robe? Did the dealer give you that to wear for the market?"

"A bit like that."

"I thought so, it's a good robe!"

Milon didn't want to tell his life story. He stared at the passing fields, farmland and trees, and was silent.

It was almost evening when the wagon arrived at a big estate, built in Roman style. In the centre was a wide paved courtyard, surrounded by buildings. On one side Milon noticed an elegantly built villa, with splendid gardens. Here Andarius, a veteran Roman commander, lived with his wife Pyrra. After an active life at war in the East, serving Caesar, he now spent a quiet and pleasant retirement. He didn't manage the estate himself. His steward strictly controlled the countless slaves and servants, and his granary and wool yields multiplied from year to year.

A groom hurried out to meet the wagon and tend the horses. The steward turned to the two newcomers. "You can wash the dust from your face and body over there at the well. I'll take you to see your future master to start work soon."

He turned towards the villa and climbed a few steps to the terrace where Andarius rested at this time of day. He found him with his wife, listening to the droning chant of a slave girl, who accompanied her song with a few notes plucked from the strings of a lyre. When the steward had greeted the couple, he told them, "If it would please you, sir, I could lead in the two slaves I bought in Alexandria today. One of them will serve in the villa; the other, for the time being, as a shepherd in the field. Would your lordship please choose which one should serve in the house?"

Andarius glanced over to Pyrra. "Would you prefer to see them tonight or decide in the morning?"

"Oh, do bring them here! Let's see what you bought in Alexandria."

When the steward returned to the courtyard, the slaves had washed off the travel dust and were about to dress. "A loin cloth is enough," he said. "With slaves it's the muscles, not the clothes, which count."

As they approached the steps to the terrace they paused and, seeing the master and mistress, threw themselves down respectfully, their foreheads touching the lowest step. The steward brought them up and introduced them.

"This dark one is called Lesco, strongly built, he could have been taken on the galley service. He's served in Alexandria and knows housework. This one is Milon, a Greek, who was on a boat, but also in service in Pompeii."

Andarius studied them for a moment with a searching eye. "Fetch me some flowers from the garden. Bring them here," he ordered.

Quickly Lesco was down the steps, while Milon hesitated a moment, looking round, then he followed him. Lesco soon returned with a big bouquet. He took a water jug, which stood on the terrace, hastily pushed the flowers into it and stood them on the stone table. A little later Milon returned with a few yellow roses in his hand. Seeing that Lesco has already taken the last jug, he moved hesitantly towards the mistress. With a friendly bow of his head he presented the roses to her. The master laughed aloud at the slave's offer of roses to the Roman patrician lady.

"Pyrra you have a new admirer! He introduces himself rosily, but as a house servant he might only feed you and starve me. We will keep the dark one, Lesco."

He turned to Lesco and said, "Taking the empty jug and knowing how to use it made me choose you."

But as they departed Lesco heard the mistress remark that she would have preferred Milon, in spite of his shyness. This annoyed Lesco. Pyrra knew well that, having made his decision, Andarius wasn't going to take it back.

The steward told Milon to give his colourful robe to Lesco and wear his worn-out tunic instead. This was good enough for a shepherd.

There were many slaves on this estate. They mostly worked in the fields, with others in the stables, the house, the yard and the kitchen. They all shared common sleeping quarters above the stables, where they slept on straw mattresses. Only the housekeeper, a long-serving old slave, lived next to the steward in a room in the villa. Great guard dogs kept watch in the yard. They would bark at the slightest sound in the night and could tear any fleeing slave to pieces on the spot. The two newcomers were quartered at the furthest end of the long room.

The following evening, as they lay on their straw mattresses in the dark, Lesco said to Milon, "I'm glad I got house service. The master and mistress aren't troublesome and I'm at the source of good things. Today I've eaten roast goose. How did you fare, Milon?"

"I tended the sheep in the field. The supervisor gave me a strong stick to fend off wild dogs that might attack the flock. I ate bread and fruit, but I had a good midday rest in the shade of the olive trees while the sun was scorching. There's thick desert bush along the edge of the field, where wild dogs could suddenly appear, but I have a sheep dog beside me and he keeps good watch."

While Milon was describing this, Lesco thought to himself, *What miserable work! I've drawn the better straw. Hopefully everything will stay as it is, if only the mistress doesn't want to swap him for me one day.*

Lesco had not forgotten that she would have preferred Milon.

A Strange Encounter

One hot day Milon was resting out in the field. He'd eaten his meagre bread under a group of trees. The sheep lay gathered together round him in the shade. Some of them nibbled a little further away at the half-dry grass tussocks. Milon was almost asleep, when suddenly the grazing sheep came racing towards the trees, bleating loudly, tripping over each other as they ran. In no time the whole flock was off, taking to its heels in wild confusion. The sheep dog chased them in vain, barking after the terrified animals, but they wouldn't stop.

Milon sprang to his feet in shock. Seizing his stick, he gazed around. Had a wild dog frightened them? At first he couldn't see what had startled them; he just watched as they fled, raising a cloud of dust behind them on the dry ground. *Should I chase after them?* he wondered. *Or stay here and leave it to the dog to drive them back?*

He turned in the direction of the bushes where the noise had come from. Then his eyes widened in terror, as out of the lean desert scrub a lion emerged, fixing him in its gaze.

In a flash Milon realised, *Too late to flee! A lion leaps faster than a human stride. There's only one thing to do. Up the nearest tree!* He climbed nimbly up until he clung at last to a high branch where he felt safe. *Lions don't climb trees*, he thought.

Looking down from his perch he saw the lion approach the tree with slow, strange steps. Every time it placed its left front paw on the ground it limped heavily. Milon watched carefully. Yes, it seemed to be in great pain. Once the lion stopped, licked its paw, and then looked around searchingly. It lifted its leg and pawed the air, as if to plead for help. Then the lion looked up at the crown of the tree, and fixed its gaze on Milon again, struggling to force out a low groan. It was surely a groan of pain.

When the lion reached the shepherd's tree, it sank down, gave a long sigh and pawed again in the air with its sore paw.

For a moment Milon thought, *Could this lion be tricking me, luring me down with its pitiful gestures, only to attack me?*

But he dismissed this thought. It would have been easier for the lion to chase the sheep and catch plenty of juicy food. Milon had never seen a lion so close up. It was a strongly built male lion with a full bushy mane. Its sad gestures didn't fit with its kingly, dignified form. Milon felt compassion for this beast. It must be hurt.

Carefully he eased himself down a few branches. The lion raised its head, let out a short, trembling howl, and once again lifted its paw. Now Milon could see that the left front paw was larger than the right one. It was obviously swollen. He felt sure that the lion was asking for help; but a lion is a lion. Should he dare to go near it? Would its hunting instinct suddenly take over? Milon climbed down a few more branches. The lion responded with a low whimpering. Finally Milon decided to try and help.

With the courage of a new adventure, Milon lowered himself directly in front of the predator. The lion was lying down now, licking its outstretched swollen paw with a cautious tongue. Perhaps there was a splinter or a sharp stone, which it couldn't remove, stuck in the pad. Milon climbed quietly onto the lowest branches, keeping a careful eye on the lion. Then, summoning all his courage, he lowered himself to the ground, still ready to climb up again at any moment. The lion, as if sensing that he mustn't frighten the shepherd, remained lying down, turning on its side to wave the painful front paw in the air.

Strangely, Milon wasn't frightened any more. He was more concerned about discovering what was wrong with the lion's paw. When he was just a few steps away, Milon clicked his tongue and spoke as if he was calming a young lamb caught in a thorn thicket. Now he stood close to the lion and, with its swollen forepaw, the lion waved him nearer.

Gently Milon said, "Now … now … show me. So … yes …"

Gently but firmly he grasped the paw just behind the swelling, where it would be less sensitive. With one glance he saw what was troubling the animal: there was a long thorn stuck between the pads, which had become painfully inflamed. Carefully Milon tried to pinch the end of the thorn and pull it out. Luckily the swelling had already loosened the thorn, so it came out easily.

It was extremely long and must have caused great pain, which, after days of suffering, had driven the lion to seek human help.

Once the thorn was removed, pressure on the infected paw eased, which seemed to give the lion immediate relief. Milon stroked him gently and even ruffled his mane. The lion licked the shepherd's foot and rumbled a deep purr of pleasure. Then it seemed exhausted; it had probably not slept or hunted much since the injury. The lion rolled onto its side, rested the wounded paw over the healthy one and fell asleep.

For a moment Milon considered splitting the lion's skull with a stone; such a deed would bring him into high favour with his master, Andarius. Pyrra would appreciate the magnificent fur as a rug. But he immediately drove this ugly thought away.

He touched the sleeping lion on the mane as if to reassure him. "You're my friend now; no harm should come to you."

Then he remembered his runaway sheep. He looked far and wide, but not one white fleck of an animal could be seen. Perhaps they had run back to the sheepfold with the dog? Yes, that would be it! Milon took a few cautious steps away from the lion, which was still lying in the shade of the trees.

He took his shepherd's stick, looked back at the sleeping lion and thought, *It would be wonderful for a despised slave to have such a strong companion, friend and protector.* He would have loved to shake the lion awake and cry, "Ride with me into the wide free world where there are no supervisors, no slave dogs and no more fear!" Milon knew that these were wishful dreams — but it was good to have dreams.

But now he had to leave the lion. If the sheep had gone home without him, someone would come looking for him soon. Reluctantly he left the shaded trees, the lion and his dreams of freedom behind him. He was about to start running when he realised that his Roman master might set up a hunt to kill the poor creature if he heard about the lion. Then he wondered if the lion would come back tomorrow to visit him. Animals are often more grateful than people. If only he could tame it here secretly! He had made friends with it, after all.

No, I'll say nothing about the lion, or they will surely go after him, he thought.

The golden brown speck in the tree's shadow grew ever smaller behind him, shimmering indistinctly in the hot midday haze, as he walked away.

The Return

As he approached the estate Milon noticed a group of people rushing to meet him; among them was the supervisor with two bloodhounds on a lead. Milon heard an excited babble start up as they saw him. He realised that, when the sheep had come home alone, they must have thought he'd run away. Were the bloodhounds looking for him? As he drew nearer, Milon saw the supervisor's grim expression. It didn't bode well. The supervisor now stood before him, striking the whip handle angrily against his thigh, as though he might beat the shepherd at any moment.

He shouted, "What's the matter with you? Don't you watch your animals? You damned fool! I'll teach you to abandon your flock!" He raised his arm to punish the slave.

In a flash, Milon cried, "Oh master, a lion, a lion!"

The supervisor lowered his arm. "What! Have you seen a lion?"

"Yes, indeed, sir. That's why the sheep ran home alone."

"Tell me!" ordered the supervisor, sounding irritated but curious.

"Master, as we rested under the olive trees at midday, I suddenly heard a wild bleating from the animals. Then they were away like a whirlwind, with the dog behind them. I looked for the cause and a lion walked out of the thicket towards me. Then I ran too — up the tree. And there I had to stay, until ... until ... he could not harm me any more."

Here Milon stopped, and as the supervisor began to ask about the size and age of the animal, he answered, but he kept silent about the rest.

"I must tell our master immediately," said the supervisor, "that a lion has been seen. There have been no lions around Alexandria for many years."

On their way back, Milon was allowed to walk next to the supervisor holding the hounds. Once again he had to tell his story, and once again he kept silent about what, for him, was the highlight of his experience with the lion. That would remain his secret!

When they got back to the estate they found the sheep resting quietly in the fold, with no sign of their previous terror. Then the supervisor took Milon to see Andarius. The commander was resting on the shady terrace while his wife listened drowsily to the chant of an Egyptian slave girl. Lesco announced that the supervisor had an important message. Andarius, happy to exchange his boredom for something of interest, waved his hand. "Bring us the news, here and now."

They climbed the steps to the terrace, where not long ago the shepherd slave had carried roses. With an air of importance the supervisor announced the appearance of a lion on the estate and Milon had to tell his tale again; yet even now he hesitated to give the full story. He was afraid that they would laugh at him; that no one would believe what had really happened. While he spoke, Lesco stood by the pillar listening, and Pyrra compared Milon's slim figure, his ragged clothes and vivid retelling to the dull manners of her servant, Lesco. She still thought the shepherd would have made the more agreeable house servant.

The commander listened with growing interest; he sat up on the couch; his eyes sparkled with joy, as they had done in his younger years at the start of a battle. He had taken part in wild animal hunts many times during his long life. He especially liked to capture animals alive in traps or nets, and more than once he'd brought not only slaves, but also wild animals to Rome after a victory. What Milon had feared began to happen: Andarius ordered a carriage to be prepared immediately, so he could visit his friend, a nearby estate owner, who would certainly like to join the lion hunt. The lion might be caught or killed by tomorrow.

Milon went to repair the fences of the sheepfold. But before Andarius drove away he noticed that Pyrra hurried out to the carriage to speak to him urgently. Did she advise him against the lion hunt? It seemed that the master agreed to her request, because she said goodbye in a very friendly manner and waved after the carriage for some time. So she can't have asked him to give up the lion hunt.

Milon's question would soon be answered.

A Change of Duties

Pyrra returned to the house, and the supervisor soon beckoned to Milon from the terrace. In a few words he was told, "Go to the sleeping quarters with Lesco and swap clothes. From this evening on, *you* have to serve in the house; Lesco will be the shepherd and take over the sheep. He should stay near to the estate with the flock until this business with the lion has been resolved."

Amazed, Milon forgot to open his mouth in reply. He had enjoyed working with the sheep. Now he wouldn't be able to meet the lion by the olive trees again.

"Move!" barked the supervisor.

"Yes, sir, I'm going. Where's Lesco?"

"I've sent him ahead; he's waiting upstairs. He must explain your new tasks to you and this evening I'll introduce you."

With these words the supervisor waved him away and Milon hurried to the sleeping quarters. He found Lesco sitting, pale and tense on his mattress.

As soon as Milon appeared, Lesco shouted at him furiously, "You mean swine! You've been playing up to the mistress, to make her send me away and accept you instead. You miserable dog!"

"Lesco," Milon grieved, "I don't want to do house service. I love working with the sheep in the quiet fields by the shady trees. I can't change the will of the mistress. You know that we're slaves; that we're bought and sold like animals; sent hither and thither by our master's will."

But even these words couldn't lessen Lesco's fury. "You pretend to be innocent, you miserable devil. You invented this story of the lion to make yourself seem important. A lion in Alexandria, ridiculous! You're a liar — a lying windbag!"

Milon could say nothing in reply. He realised how someone who's determined to blind himself to the truth can twist everything. After a moment's silence he tried again to justify himself. "Lesco, your disappointment has blinded you. As truly as I see you before me, so a lion stood before me today, by the five olive trees. I didn't even tell the whole story: he had a thorn stuck in his foot which I pulled out; he licked my foot."

Lesco laughed mockingly, "Listen to this swindler! A lion has licked his foot! Why didn't you tell this to Andarius? He wouldn't have driven away in his chariot on a lion hunt then! If they don't find a lion you'll be in trouble. Then I'll tell them your fantasy story and *I'll* be the one laughing."

Grinning maliciously, Lesco tore off the robe and threw it on the floor in front of Milon, who gave him his shepherd's rags in return. Reluctantly Lesco explained the work of the house servant.

By dinnertime, Andarius still hadn't come back, so the mistress ate alone. Supervised by the housekeeper, Milon served the food, but his thoughts were elsewhere. He feared for the lion's life and freedom.

Late that night the master returned, his chariot guided by a bright moon. He told his wife, "My friend has a Roman captain staying as a guest. His soldiers are waiting for new orders from Rome, so they have time on their hands. He's happy for some of them to join the lion hunt, as long as the lion is sent to the arena in Alexandria for the autumn animal fights. He heard, a few days earlier, that a lion had appeared and frightened some farmers in this neighbourhood, so it's probably the same one."

Pyrra was relieved to hear that her husband would organise the hunt but not take part himself. Then she thanked him for agreeing to change the house servant.

Up in the slave's sleeping quarters that evening, there was only one topic: Milon and the lion. Only one slave didn't take part, but lay brooding and silent on his straw bed. He didn't say a word about pulling out the thorn either, which Milon hadn't told the others. He was afraid that, if it were true, Milon would receive even more attention and honour. Inwardly Lesco burned with fury and hated Milon for taking his pleasant role as house servant. Now he was exposed to the tormenting heat and sandy winds; he had only meagre shepherd's bread to eat, and he felt that he'd almost die of boredom out in the fields. One thought went round and round his mind: how can I remove Milon from the villa and get back my rightful position? He decided one thing for sure: if the lion was neither caught nor seen, he would tell his masters that Milon had invented the story to make himself seem important and ingratiate himself as a house servant. Then Milon would face the fury of Andarius, who had arranged a lion hunt on the lie of a slave. Maybe he would be beaten to death. Lesco would certainly return to his old service. So, for now, Lesco kept his feelings hidden, but waited to take his revenge.

Milon had to serve longer this evening because of the master's late return. He was the last one back to sleeping quarters, but when he arrived many slaves gathered round his bed in the dark, full of questions. He warded them off, saying, "I want to sleep! Leave me in peace."

Next to him lay Lesco, pretending to sleep soundly. When they heard the steps of the supervisor on the stairs, everyone flitted like cats to their beds and silence descended on the room. The supervisor entered with a glimmering oil lamp. Walking around he checked that no bed was empty. He stopped next to Milon and spoke in a friendly manner, which he seldom used for the slaves, "Now, Milon, we'll have your lion by the mane soon. Tomorrow is the hunt. If you like you can accompany our master."

"As you please, sir, but given a choice, I'd rather stay at home. The mistress has given me orders for some special tasks tomorrow."

"So stay at home," the supervisor laughed cheerfully, "but I'll go with them. A lion hunt is a rare event in this land."

Suddenly he turned round to Lesco, shook him by the shoulder and asked mockingly, "How do you like it with the sheep and the crispy shepherd's bread?"

Lesco answered obsequiously, "Sir, everywhere I fulfil my duty for your satisfaction."

"Watch out," said the supervisor, "perhaps the lion will eat you tomorrow before we catch him in the net; then I will have you whipped as a punishment!" He laughed at his bad joke and the slaves laughed with him. Soon they heard him descend the stairs again and after some whispering all was silent. Sleep settled over the tired slaves.

One of them, however, tossed restlessly on his straw bed. It was Lesco, whose soul burned even more deeply with bitterness after the gloating laughter of his comrades.

The Day of the Lion Hunt

At dawn the next day, beaters for the hunt headed off through the palm scrub. Milon saw Andarius drive away in a wagon, with the supervisor, a groom and two runners, who would make useful messengers. For a while he gazed after them, thinking, *I hope the lion has already left the area. His foot must still be sore; he's not ready to run fast.*

Milon felt like a traitor when he thought that the lion could fall into the hands of the Romans, dead or alive. The hours passed. Every time a dog barked, Milon sprang to the terrace to look for arrivals.

It was past noon when one of the runners brought a message to Pyrra from her husband: "The lion is caught. The master requests a celebration meal for ten guests."

This meant a lot of work for the kitchen and for Milon. He just had time to ask how they had captured the lion, and the runner reported eagerly, "The dogs tracked him into the thicket. Then the hunters encircled him with long nets. They didn't throw spears because he wasn't very fierce, but they closed in on him from three sides, with nets spread wide, and soon he was trapped. Now he's in the wagon on the way to Alexandria, where he'll be kept for the autumn games."

Milon felt torn as he listened to these words: now the lion was caught Lesco could no longer accuse him of lying; but what a pity that the lion hadn't been able to escape to freedom. But there was no time to ask further questions; the housekeeper and kitchen servants were in a great commotion. How could they prepare a festive meal for ten lion hunters so quickly?

When the hunters drove into the courtyard at sunset, Pyrra and the housekeeper greeted them joyfully. Andarius proudly handed his wife a strand of the lion's mane. The commander's face, usually so stern, was alive with laughter. A little away from the house, by the sheepfold, Lesco stood in the shade of a tree and watched. He clenched his fist when he saw how Andarius presented Milon to the Roman captain as the hero of the day, because he'd discovered the lion. He saw how Andarius pressed something into the slave's hand, and how the slave bowed humbly in thanks.

The Roman captain had brought his officers with him. As Milon, nimble and light-footed, carried the dishes and heavy wine jugs between the guests, he listened to find out more about the hunt. At first it was the main subject of conversation: how the lion, unexpectedly, showed little aggression when he became caught in the nets; although he had desperately tried to free himself as his feet were being bound, and one of the hunters had torn a calf muscle.

Over the course of the evening, the talk moved on to war and new Roman conquests. Milon listened, following everything closely, while still making sure that the guests' cups were never left empty. Next the conversation turned to a strange group of people who had appeared some time ago in Rome, and had not been welcomed by Caesar.

"What kind of people?" asked Pyrra.

The Roman captain explained, "They call themselves Christians and believe in one god, who died on the cross in Jerusalem, under Tiberius Caesar."

"What does Caesar have against them?" Pyrra asked. "The Romans worship many gods and have even made room for foreign gods in their temples."

"Well, the god of the Christians seems to be different from other gods," the captain continued. "They say he lived on earth as a man and then rose from the dead as a god. They call him a 'god of love', which is why the Christians don't want to be soldiers or to kill. But Rome and Caesar need soldiers; so if the Christian god became mighty in the Roman Empire, the whole empire would fall. Caesar knows that, which is why he suppresses and persecutes them."

Andarius said, "In the legion I last commanded there were a number of soldiers from Egypt who called themselves Christians. They stood out as disciplined soldiers, but they stayed away from sacrifices to the gods. I let them have their way. One of them explained to me that they followed the principle: 'Give to Caesar what belongs to Caesar, and to God what belongs to God.' That seemed sensible and I had no reason to interfere. But I also heard that there are some hermits who live in the wilderness and choose to fast, living only for their Christian god and despising the world. If this practice were to spread, our lands would soon be empty of people. So I say, 'Long live our Roman gods, Mars, Venus and Jupiter, and may Roman might and wealth continue!'" With these words, Andarius raised his cup and they all applauded him heartily.

Now the conversation turned again to hunting stories, but Milon thought, *The Romans have their gods who make them rich and mighty; for poor slaves there are none, and the gods of Greece are far away. I never knew my father and mother, who might have told me of a god of slaves. Not one of my fellow slaves worships a Roman god.*

Sadness filled him as he leaned, tired, against one of the pillars in the open hall, holding a wine jug. The light from the flaming torches flickered and dimmed over the feasting Romans. Milon watched how midges and moths dived into the flames and were burned. *The Romans are the proud flames and we slaves are the midges and moths*, he thought. Then he lifted his eyes to the stars and remembered the silent nights when, as a boy, he had herded sheep near Delphi and knew no other script than the book of the stars. Then he had imagined a god above the stars, who seemed so infinitely far away that he had never dared to pray or speak to him.

Suddenly the housekeeper was beside him, elbowing him in the ribs and hissing, "You're dreaming! The cups are almost empty. Do your rounds."

Milon gave himself a shake. The jug had almost fallen. Paying more attention to his work, he left his dreams of moths, stars and gods for the rest of the evening.

It was gone midnight when the hunting group parted. Milon helped to harness the horses and soon the great wheels thundered across the paved courtyard and away into the night. As he walked to the sleeping quarters he took the silver coin which Andarius had given him from his pocket. In the moonlight he stopped to study the image of Caesar of Rome, who was said to be like the immortal gods. Would this coin bring him unexpected luck, as the golden Titus had? Where could he store it? As a slave, he had neither cupboard nor locker; under his mattress seemed the safest place. He would sleep on the Caesar coin, and during the day he could carry it around with him in his girdle to look at and enjoy.

Betrayed and Beaten

The days passed. Lesco's monotonous work as a shepherd outside in heat or storms, and the meagre bread and fruit he took with him in his leather bag, became evermore unbearable. Over weeks of brooding, he hatched a plan to have Milon removed from house service. During his time as a house slave, Lesco had noticed that the mistress' ring and bracelet always lay in the bathroom early in the morning. She only put them on after washing in the morning. He decided to wait for an opportunity to creep unnoticed into the house, then the mistress' precious ring would disappear, and Milon would be accused of stealing it.

His chance came one morning, when Lesco was passing the villa, watchful eyed. He noticed that the housekeeper had gathered the servants on the terrace to receive their orders for the day. Like a cat Lesco disappeared round the corner of the house, slipped through the backdoor and entered the quiet rooms. The master and mistress had not yet risen. He paused for a moment outside the bathroom and listened; nothing stirred. Silently he drew the curtain aside and stepped in.

The mistress' jewels lay in the polished bowl of a shell, with a few hair clips beside them. His hand shook with fear and greed as he reached for the ring, with its blood-red gem. His fingers clutched the jewel. Sweat rolled from his brow; he brushed it aside mechanically as he slipped out of the room. Outside no one had seen the slightest sign of his theft. In his clenched hand the ruby glowed like fire. Lesco passed the sheepfold, glancing back at the terrace. The housekeeper was still speaking to the servants. He hurried to the slave kitchen below the sleeping quarters. He had deliberately not taken any bread, giving him a reason to return. Barefooted, he flitted noiselessly up the stone steps, lifted the head end of Milon's straw mattress to hide the

94

ring below, and noticed with surprise that a silver coin already lay hidden there.

Sneering, he laid the ring beside it, and hissed, "You'll be in good company!"

Then he let the mattress fall back, gloating at the thought that the silver coin would bear further witness to Milon's hiding place and treasure gathering. Again no one saw him enter the kitchen, take his bread and hurry out to the pasture with the sheep. On other days he had left the herding to the dog and lagged lazily behind. But today he threw stones after the sheep, which made the dog excited, driving the flock more quickly towards the five olive trees.

When Pyrra rose, her slave girl, Baarla, helped her with her morning wash. She handed her the golden bracelet from the shell bowl and reached for the ring. It was not there. She lifted the bowl. "Where is your ring, my lady? Is it in the bedroom perhaps?"

"No," answered Pyrra, "I always leave my jewels in this shell at night. Isn't it there?"

"No, my lady. Could it have fallen on the floor?"

Baarla was already searching all the corners of the room with a feather brush — in vain. Pyrra flew about the bedroom, although she knew for certain that she'd left the ring in the bathroom last night. The jewel was nowhere to be found. Pyrra broke into tears. The ring was a precious gift from Andarius after his last victorious campaign. Shocked, Baarla called the housekeeper, who helped them search everywhere, with an increasingly anxious expression. It became clear that the ring had been stolen.

When Andarius heard of the loss he ordered for all the slaves in the house to be gathered immediately. The supervisor searched the slaves' clothing meticulously, armed with his whip. No one knew anything about the lost ring. It was nowhere to be found.

Then the housekeeper said to Pyrra and Andarius, "We should give the thief the chance to return the ring, and if we find the thief he should be severely punished. The house slaves are all here. Those who are in the field can be questioned this evening.

Please allow me to whip the guilty one and sell him as a galley slave in the market."

"Do as you wish. The ring must be found!" barked Andarius.

Again the supervisor gathered the slaves with a loud whistle. He ordered them to search the house and courtyard once more. Towards evening, when the field slaves returned from their work, the supervisor had all the mattresses carried from the sleeping quarters down to the courtyard. Slaves sometimes hid stolen objects in them. Some were already busy tearing the mattresses apart when a cry was heard from the sleeping quarters: "Bring the sacks back, I've found the ring!"

Upstairs the supervisor stood next to Milon's straw mattress. Under it lay the silver coin and, beside it, the ring. He gave orders for Milon to be fetched from the villa. After checking that the ring was undamaged, he put it back, next to the silver coin. Forcefully flexing the leather whip in both hands, he waited for the culprit.

White-faced, Milon appeared; the slave who had brought him had already told him what they'd found. As he approached, the supervisor pointed the whip at the coin and the ring and shouted, "Damned scoundrel! Confess that *you* are the thief."

Milon stared at the ring under his bed as if struck by lightening. Horrified, he fixed his eyes upon the sparkling red ruby stone and stammered, "Master, I know nothing ..."

The leather whip whistled past his face with terrible force. A kick of the foot threw him to the ground. Mercilessly, full of pent-up rage, the supervisor beat the writhing slave on the ground, until streams of blood and dust covered Milon's clothes. Swearing, he delivered a few more kicks, then he beckoned the watching servants, who stood paralysed with fear, to throw the battered body into the house prison. Four of them lifted the groaning human bundle and carried him across the courtyard.

There was a spare stall in the pigsty, which sometimes served as a prison cell for lazy or unruly slaves. Here Milon was locked in.

Not long after, Lesco returned, late on purpose, with the

sheep from the field. A groom met him, eager to tell him the news. The whipped thief lay in the pigsty and could expect the worst punishment. He was sure to be sold as a galley slave. Lesco listened with pretend calm, but a gleam of triumph shone in his eyes. *It worked!* he thought. Revenge was complete. Once the sheep were in the fold, he strolled indifferently towards the slave house. As they gathered in the kitchen, he asked to hear every detail of the event again: the search and the discovery of the ring. It had all happened as he had hoped it would.

Shortly after his return, the housekeeper called for Lesco. "Go and wash yourself thoroughly and ask for house servant's clothes. You will go back to your former service. Old Libo will be the shepherd. Give him your bag."

In his thoughts Lesco was jubilant. *How quickly fate can be changed when you know how to direct it!* Out loud he replied to the housekeeper, "Sir, I'll be quick, and I'm happy to be serving in the house again to your satisfaction."

Soon Lesco stood on the terrace, sparkling clean and clothed, serving his master and mistress in the cool evening breeze with a friendly smile, as if he'd never been a shepherd.

Pyrra was strangely quiet. From time to time she looked at her ring, shining red in the light of the oil lamps. Again and again she saw the image, which she'd glimpsed through a half-open door onto the courtyard, of bearers dragging the blood-covered Milon into the pigsty; he, whose friendly, attentive service she had valued so much.

Had the seductive red glow of the stone confused the poor slave, until he couldn't resist taking it? Whichever way she saw it, the ring gave her no answer. Milon was surely not an ordinary thief, or had his eyes, which were so often sad, deceived her? She would have imagined Lesco much more capable of theft, with his sly sideways glances. *But people are mysterious; they often have an inner and outer face which don't always match*, thought Pyrra.

Andarius said unexpectedly, as if he'd read her thoughts, "What a shame. He seemed to be a loyal fellow. I was about to congratulate you on your choice. At least we could get the other one back again." With this, their conversation about Milon ended.

Late in the evening, when the slave girl, Baarla, accompanied her mistress into the bedroom, she asked, "Mistress, would you allow me to go and wash the wounds of the slave, Milon, in the stall?"

"Why would you do this?"

"My mother taught me that sick and wretched people should be helped. She was a Christian and always said that all people are brothers and sisters. I was ten years old when she died, but these words have stayed with me."

"What a strange teaching," pondered Pyrra, "but go to Milon and take him something to drink. There have been famous Romans, too, who have made themselves rich from other people's property and have never been punished. There's just one thing I don't understand: he would know how this loss would affect me, but what was he going to do with the ring? It just doesn't add up. But do go over; I feel sorry for the poor fellow."

After telling the housekeeper, Baarla took a jug, a basin and an oil lamp and went through the courtyard to the stalls. A dog barked as she pulled out the wedge from the door of the stall where Milon lay. Holding up the light, she shone it into the dark and stinking stall. Unmoving, but breathing heavily, Milon lay on the filthy floor. Baarla was shocked when the light fell on his swollen, bleeding face.

"Water!" he gasped when he saw the jug.

Baarla helped to lift his head and held the jug to his lips. He gulped it with deep drafts. In one corner Baarla found a pile of straw and slipped some under his head. She washed the blood from his face with a wet cloth, gave him more to drink, and dampened his clothes where the dried blood of his wounds had stuck them to his body. She pushed grapes from a large bunch into his mouth as if he was a helpless child. He ate them slowly.

At last Milon could speak again and asked almost inaudibly, "Who sent you to me?"

She answered softly, "I follow the command of Christ, as my mother taught me."

For a while he gazed wide-eyed into the flame of the oil lamp. "Is your Christ a god of the slaves?"

"He's a god of all people, not only slaves. My mother taught me that he died for *all* people, so that truth and love may live on earth."

Milon let his head fall back on the straw, searching for words. "If Christ died for the truth then he knows that I'm innocent. I never touched Pyrra's ring. Never!"

Exhausted he closed his eyes. Baarla was shocked by these words. She had heard all the evidence of the theft. Was he lying now out of weakness, after his beating, or had there been a mistake? With a linen cloth she dried the tears that welled up under Milon's closed eyes, mixed with blood and sweat. She whispered, "Sleep now. The pain will go. I'll look after you and you'll get well again."

She rose gently and disappeared with the light. As she pushed the door wedge in again Milon felt a quiet, warming brightness remain with him in the dark. He scarcely felt the burning wounds any more. Even his bitterness towards Lesco who, as he well knew, had so shamefully betrayed him, faded away. Quiet and peace embraced him. He saw the image of Baarla's gentle eyes shining in the lamplight. Dreams soothed his pain, until suffering and injustice were drowned in a deep sleep.

The Slave Market in Alexandria

A few days later, the supervisor gave orders to prepare a wagon for the journey to Alexandria. The steward was going shopping in the city and would take this opportunity to sell the thief. When Baarla heard this was happening so quickly she hurried to the stall with bread and water. She found no one inside; Milon, already washed and dressed in a clean cloth, sat in a corner of the slaves' kitchen, eating boiled millet, his food for the day. No one said a word to him. Even the cook, who had been fond of Milon, treated him with contempt and couldn't look him in the eye while she filled his bowl.

Baarla walked slowly back to the villa, deep in thought. She had slept restlessly, wondering about Milon and the ring. Was he innocent? He had sounded so clear and truthful when he said, "I never touched Pyrra's ring!" No, Milon hadn't lied to her. Should she speak to Pyrra about it? But who was the guilty one? Pyrra hadn't yet called her to help her wash, and she couldn't wake the mistress to plead for a slave.

Outside in the courtyard she could hear the wagon arriving. Baarla hurried out. The steward sat at the front; a groom tied empty baskets to the wagon. Now Milon climbed on board with bound hands, and a fellow slave tied him with a rope to the wagon to prevent escape.

Baarla longed to cry out, "Let Milon stay for one more day! The search must continue. He is innocent!" But such words would have only earned her scorn and derision.

Suddenly one of the baskets dropped off the wagon onto the cobbles. This gave Baarla a chance. Quick as a flash she stepped forward to pick up the basket. While it was being tied back on, Baarla approached the prisoner and whispered, "Milon, do you know who took Pyrra's ring?"

"Lesco!"

She whispered, "Farewell! I know you're innocent. I will pray for you!" Then the wheels rattled and the two slaves lost sight of each other.

As Baarla turned back to the house, she saw Lesco on the terrace. He was staring at the archway through which the wagon had disappeared, spellbound. Then a smile spread over his normally tense face and in it Baarla read triumph and satisfaction.

"Yes, it's him," Baarla groaned, but she couldn't call back the wagon. It rolled on to Alexandria.

The slave market in the great city was a daily event, as trade came in from the sea as well as the land. There were several divisions in the great square where it was held: one for clever young slaves to be house servants; another for skilled workmen; one for field labourers and carriers; then a smaller group where rebellious thieves and criminal slaves were offered at a cheap price. These were used as rowers on galleys, or for pulling barges up the Nile. Milon was taken to this section, his face and body still showing signs of the whip. He looked around and soon noticed a trader bargaining with the steward who had brought him. They came to an agreement, as Milon could see by the fall of silver coins into the steward's hand.

The steward left without a word, and the dealer who had bought him approached as his new master. He had already examined him thoroughly. Now, with his rough hand, he rubbed the raw whip wounds on Milon's back. "They'll soon be better!" He loosened him from the stake to which he'd been tied, and fastened him to a chain with two other slaves who'd also been bought.

"Get moving! To the harbour!" he commanded and pushed them forward. One of the slaves, who had served in Alexandria, knew the way to the harbour. He called himself Rano. The dealer let them go ahead and he strolled behind them.

Rano said quietly to his comrades, "Let's hope it's not the galleys; we'll be chained to benches and have to row for the rest of our lives."

At the harbour, the dealer directed them to a ship named *Roma*.

"A sailing ship, not a galley!" whispered Rano joyfully.

"We could be sailors," added the other one, Pinaro.

On board they were released from their chains and their hands were untied. The ship was to leave Alexandria the following morning, so there was cargo to be carried on board, piled up and tied.

Rano stayed close to Milon while they worked and asked, "Those wounds on your body show that you've been whipped recently. Did you try to escape like me?"

"No, I was wrongly accused as a thief and whipped for what I didn't do."

Rano replied bitterly, "Haven't you learnt that a slave is always guilty and always in the wrong?"

Milon was silent. He thought to himself, *Here's someone who knows the truth.*

With this thought in mind, he could bear whatever came to him with more confidence. Something deep inside of him had changed since Baarla had cared for him that night in the stall. For all these years he'd lived in fear of what worse things could happen to him as a slave. Now this fear was gone. Baarla had passed on some strength from the hidden god, who had died for slaves as well. Had she not whispered to him when they parted, "I know you're innocent"? This certainty, that someone knew the truth, made him glad, even now that a dark, unknown future lay ahead.

While they worked, Rano told Milon that he'd tried to escape to freedom, back to Rhodes, where he, his parents and siblings had been stolen by pirates. He had never heard from them since. Milon could speak his beloved Greek with Rano.

Night fell over the city and sea. The slaves were locked in the hold so they couldn't escape during the night. Milon lay between bundles of goods. His tired body still throbbed, with a stinging pain in his muscles and bones. As he lay in the dark, the only slave awake, he thought that the silver Caesar coin had not brought him luck after all. Even Athena was lost to him now, because his belt had been taken away. This ship would sail close to Rome; maybe he would go once more to the city where Caesar lived. Would he perhaps meet him face to face one day?

Arriving in Rome

Milon and his two companions soon discovered that the rest of the ship's crew had long since settled in, and that even the ship's slaves saw them as newcomers and strangers. They were the only ones on board who had come from criminal's corner and been told nothing of what lay ahead. They were given the meanest work; they were the slaves of slaves.

After a few days the weather became stormy and the sails were lowered; high waves swept over the deck. In one bleak moment Milon was seized by a flooding wave and almost washed overboard. Yet something within him made him hold tightly to a rescuing rope as the deck slid away beneath his feet. After several hours the storm subsided, the sails filled with wind again and the sun's rays shone through the retreating storm clouds. *A sea voyage is like human life,* Milon thought as he watched the chase and splendour of the clouds.

Weeks later the ship entered the harbour of Portus Augusti, where he'd once looked a fine figure on a chariot and paid with gold. One time in his life, for a few hours, he had been the master and relished the joy of respect and freedom.

Upon their arrival the three slaves from Alexandria were bound together on a heavy chain. They weren't allowed to help unload the cargo. The dealer, who was also the captain, went ashore, returning on board during the day with a Roman trader. The three Egyptian slaves were brought before him. Their age and shape seemed to please him. After the purchase he led them off, still bound by their heavy chain.

This trader bought slaves for special purposes in the city of Rome. This time he'd been looking for young men to compete in the great games of the arena, where men and animals often faced each other. They must be nimble and strong and, as it didn't matter whether they lived or died, criminal slaves were especially appropriate. They were often daring and cunning, showing a ferocity that was prized in these games.

Milon and his companions were taken to a vault near the Colosseum in Rome, where they were to be imprisoned for one week until the start of the games. They still didn't know what was going to happen to them. The large room, where some prisoners were already resting on benches and pallets, had a courtyard where they could go outside during the day. The food was rich and strong, quite different from the usual prison fare. The inmates were fed to strengthen them, to fill them with power for the games. Milon and his two companions, like the others, had their chains and fetters removed. Day and night guards stood before the massive oak door.

A prisoner asked Milon, "Have you killed someone, to bring you to this hall of death?"

Startled, Milon asked, "Hall of death! What do you mean?"

"Do you see that barred gate over there? A long corridor leads straight from it into the arena. There, in one week's time, we may be slaughtered for the entertainment of the Romans. Those who remain may be freed."

Speechless, Milon's eyes roamed the room. Yes, he now saw that everyone gathered here must know! Their faces mostly shone with fear; others showed a grim determination to fight until the last breath; some showed a dull resignation, given over to death. Almost all were strongly built young men, selected to fight in the arena.

Milon's throat tightened at the thought that his bitter slave life would end in such a terrible way. Was there no justice on earth? Then it was not ruled by good gods alone. Or could the words that an old slave had told him once be true? "The gods have gone to the stars, it is demons who wreak havoc on earth! All will end in darkness!"

Milon sat alone with his back against the wall and closed his eyes. Thoughts welled up, struggling within him. Suddenly he became aware of whispering from behind. In a dark corner of the dimly lit vault, where only a little light shone from the courtyard opening, Milon saw a group of about five people, among them a woman. A bearded old man with white hair stood by the wall, speaking in a low voice. Those who surrounded him held their arms crossed over their chests. Milon was curious.

He crept closer to the group, unnoticed, and listened. He could barely hear the murmur of the old man, but he heard his drawn-out last words: "*In nomine Christi*, Amen."

Milon pricked up his ears. Could these be Christians? Noticing him nearby they quietly withdrew into the courtyard, except for the old man who stayed in the corner.

They look like a family, thought Milon. *The grandfather, the parents and their two sons.* Their clothing was not like the slaves

The old man sat on a wooden pallet by the wall. Milon hesitated to approach him, since his eyes were closed; he seemed to be deep in thought. So he strolled out into the courtyard, hoping to speak to one of the other four.

The courtyard was surrounded by high walls, part of the arena buildings. Stone blocks served as seats. Milon saw the family sitting together in the almost shadowless glare of the midday sun. He approached the group and greeted them. "*Salvete, in nomine Christi* — I greet you in the name of Christ!"

Surprised, they looked at the stranger. The father of the family rose quickly, gripped Milon's hands and whispered, "Are you our brother in Christ?"

"I would like to be," he answered, thinking of Baarla.

They invited him to sit with them and asked him why he was there. Milon found the story easy to tell because they listened to his sufferings, joys and thoughts in a way that no one had before. His life stood before him, image by image. He felt as if the events of the last days, weeks and months had been guided by an unseen hand, which had led him here to these people in the vault.

When he told them of his last ordeal with Andarius, they fell silent. Milon's new friends were deeply touched by his life as a slave. He took courage and asked what had led them, as Romans, to be here.

The father began, "My name is Marius, this is my wife Dina, and my sons Philippus and Bartholomeus. We are a Roman family of master builders, descended from Vero. My father, who is inside, has built many fine villas on the hills of Rome, as well as designing public buildings. One evening, when he was building the temple of Jupiter and the workers had already gone home, my father was looking for a lost tool when he met a group of people, who had gathered secretly behind the piled-up marble blocks. One of them began to speak with a passion that my father had never heard before. He was called Paul the apostle. At first my father was annoyed and wanted to drive the crowd away from the temple precincts, but as he listened closer, the stranger's powerful speech took root in his heart. He sat down on one of the nearby blocks and listened to the message of Christ, the son of God, who had appeared to Paul outside the city of Damascus, risen from the dead. My father stayed, listening until nightfall; the old gods no longer spoke in his heart.

"From then on he went to a new meeting place each evening, which they chose the night before; the Christians didn't feel safe from their enemies in Rome. My father soon became a member of this community of Christians and a friend of the messenger, Paul. He put the images and symbols of the old gods away in our house and brought us up in a new belief. Then the Romans started to spread hatred against Christians. We gathered secretly at night every week in our house because it was set in a great park with several entrances.

"The persecution has got worse under this Caesar and our lives have been threatened. Some brothers and sisters have died as martyrs. We began to gather more and more in underground caves, in the catacombs." Marius paused, as if held spellbound by an inner vision.

Milon asked, "What are these catacombs? Are they not graves?"

"Yes, the catacombs are underground graveyards, carved out of soft rock. They're long passages, with burial chambers on each side where the dead are laid. The Romans shy away from the dead; they don't go into the catacombs, except for burials, and especially not at night. We Christians do not fear the dead; their bodies belong to the earth, but their souls go another way. The Risen One has brought them light in the realm of death.

"We chose a deserted catacomb where all the chambers were walled up. We carved out a room in the furthest passage as a chapel, and there we gathered. On one wall my father painted Jesus Christ, with his twelve disciples at the last supper. For a long time, we held our services to God undisturbed in candlelit silence, deep beneath the noisy city. Then one day, disaster struck. A senator of the city council heard that my father had befriended the Christians. For a long time he'd been jealous of our house in its beautiful park. A spy told him about a special festival that we planned to celebrate at our house. We'd finished the ceremony and the visitors had left by the time he arrived to attack us. But when his soldiers searched our house they found signs of our celebration of the holy meal and they threw us into this vault. We don't know what will happen to us. Relatives are trying to free us, but so far no messages have reached us."

Marius fell silent. It seemed strange to Milon that a once free and noble Roman would share his life story with a slave. Now Marius turned to one of his sons and said, "Philippus, go and fetch Grandfather so he can meet our new friend Milon."

Old Vero greeted Milon as a brother. From then on he always sat with the family and he trusted them completely. Only now, in these days in prison, did Milon come to understand what it meant to be human. He had many questions, and he always received illuminating answers. He especially wanted to ask Vero about the old gods and their temples. If they had lived, where were they now?

Vero replied, "You ask wisely, Milon. I will try to tell you what I understand about it in simple words." They settled on the stone blocks and Vero began.

"All ancient people — Persians, Egyptians, Greeks and Jews — had their temples and rituals, and God had revealed part of his wisdom to them. The Persians worshipped the Creator, the 'light of the world', in the Sun; they made offerings to him on fire altars. The Egyptians called him Osiris and hoped to enter his realm after death. The Greeks knew him as the sun god, Apollo. But in changing times, the truth needs to wear different clothing. What the ancient peoples called their gods, we Christians may call 'angels'. All these old religions were heralds of the approaching Christ.

"When Jesus was baptised in the river Jordan, the spirit of God entered into the man and lived in him on earth among people. This is a unique and great wonder: that the Creator came down to earth as the son of God. People today, and probably for a long time to come, cannot grasp it. Even the apostle Paul, while he was still called Saul of Tarsus, couldn't accept this truth. At first he persecuted the Christians. But because Saul carried a deep sense of truth inside him, Christ rose from his death on earth and revealed himself to him. He appeared to Saul before the city of

Damascus, like lightening from the sky, face to face, and said, " Saul, Saul, why do you persecute me?" I've heard this testimony many times from Paul; the experience transformed him and he came to Rome as an apostle, now called Paul. For him no person was too lowly to hear this story and to be confirmed in its truth."

Vero was silent, and the silence embraced them all as they considered his words in their arena prison.

Milon began to understand the powerful events that had occurred in Palestine in the name of Christ, to bring a new realm of love to earth. Daily he felt how this human love had taken root in the hearts of his Christian friends. In the evening when all the prisoners lay on their straw-covered pallets, they would grope their way out into the courtyard. There, standing in a circle holding hands, they quietly repeated words spoken by the old man. *If only Baarla could be with us now*, thought Milon. *She longed to meet Christians like her mother.* Each night Vero closed the circle of prayer with the words, "To die in Christ is to live in the light. Christ be with us!"

Then they returned into the night-dark vault. Here and there a sleeper moaned in fearful dreams. Milon couldn't sleep; he listened in the darkness. From time to time he heard the distant rumble of passing wagon wheels. But what was that? Suddenly, faintly among the other noises, he thought he heard the muffled growl of animals. Listening more closely, the eerie sounds seemed to come from the passage that led to the arena. But the sounds were dulled through the walls and he couldn't recognise which animal it might be. He had heard from a fellow prisoner that animals from the wilderness, panthers and leopards, were starved before the great games, so they would spring into battle with an even greater thirst for blood.

The great games would begin in three days. For a moment Milon shivered with fear, but then warmth flowed from his hands to his heart, as it had when he stood with his friends in the courtyard repeating the old man's words: "To die in Christ is to live in the light ..." The muffled sounds blended with the rumble of wheels and the groans of the sleeping prisoners.

The Great Games

The following days dragged by. Time stretched with the horrible uncertainty of what was to come. The noises of wagons and people sounded busier and louder over the courtyard wall. Early on the day of the great games, many of the prisoners left their food untouched as they crouched miserably on their pallets.

Suddenly the gate opened, and the prison warder stepped in with the leader of the games and some armed men. He gathered the prisoners for selection. Taking a wax tablet and pointing to Pinaro, Rano, Milon and Philippus, he said, "These four are young and strong, take them to the back cages!"

"Pardon, circus master," said the warder, "this one here, Philippus Vero by name, comes from a reputable Roman family. No final judgement has yet been passed for him. I cannot give him to you yet."

"Well then," said the circus master, "three are enough for the cages."

Milon said goodbye to his friends and they whispered words of courage to him. The old grandfather said, "Oh Milon, if only I could die for you! I would do it happily!"

Then the armed guards led Milon with his ship companions through the long dark passage, lit only by narrow slits in the wall. They were brought to a bathroom to be prepared for the Roman public. After washing their beards were shaved and their bodies were rubbed with oil. A clean white linen cloth was bound around their loins instead of their tattered rags. Strangely, it almost seemed festive to Milon, to be prepared for a gruesome death. He could already hear the noise of the thronging crowd, which had begun to fill the arena since early that morning.

There were guided to a stone bench in an anteroom, shackles

attached to an iron chain were fastened round their ankles, and a warder gave them a jug of wine and chunks of bread.

"Drink for courage and strength," he said, "then your legs will be swift when you have to run for your life!"

While the jug was passed from hand to hand, Pinaro said, "Perhaps we'll be runners in a race. Maybe it won't be so bad after all."

"As they've made us so clean, maybe we'll be grooms for the chariot race," Rano added.

There was already a lot of bustle in the anteroom: lean sword fighters and thick-legged wrestlers appeared; jumpers performed wild leaps in the air; boxers practised shadow boxing in circles.

After a while, when the warder placed a second jug of wine before them, Pinaro asked, "What will our task be up in the arena?"

The warder grinned, saying, "You'll have to run — very fast!"

The three waiting slaves were no wiser than before. Milon noticed that they were the only ones chained. Fencers, wrestlers and boxers were usually regarded as famous celebrities when they performed before Caesar in the arena.

Milon was prepared for the worst. "Come what may, I'm ready to live or die fighting."

The crescendo of noise from the arena was suddenly silenced by trumpet calls, followed by a roar of greeting. "Caesar enters!" announced the warder, who kept a sharp eye on the three prisoners. From now on sound from the arena surged, as if it were a kettle of water kept boiling, which hissed at times as it overflowed. The warder had jumped onto the stone bench, where he could catch glimpses of the events through an opening above the wall.

More than an hour had passed, when suddenly a messenger appeared; the circus master had ordered the immediate appearance of the three prisoners. They were quickly freed from their leg-irons. With the messenger leading, the three followed and the warder came behind. Before them a gate swung open into the arena. Whip in hand, the circus master directed and called with a great flourish for one performance to follow the other without pause. Seeing the three slaves he called, "You will contend with wild animals. If you meet them with cunning and speed, or even strangle one, you might buy your freedom."

The whip stung the gate. The hinges creaked. The circus master roused them, crying, "Quick, go in! Greet Caesar and the Roman people with raised arms so that you please them."

So they ran into the arena waving, raising their arms as ordered, and bowed low towards Caesar's stand. Milon gazed at the immense crowd of people, not one of whom answered their greeting. He felt as lost and small as a grain of sand in the desert. He closed his eyes and repeated the words of old Vero.

His two companions had placed themselves in different positions, scanning round keenly to see which of the cage gates would be lifted. Milon, hearing a sudden gasp from the crowd, opened his eyes and saw two lions step out. For a moment they stood still, glaring around in the blaze of light. Pinaro and Rano began to run to the other side of the arena, and the lions chased after the fleeing figures. Wildly excited, the crowd screamed as the beasts drew nearer to their prey. Horrified, Milon saw Pinaro fall to the ground under the claws of one lion. He rolled over in the sand, then rose, bleeding, to run again in the opposite direction.

Milon stood unmoving. He lost sight of Pinaro now as Rano, in deadly haste, came running towards him, zigzagging cleverly. Was he looking for help? Milon prepared to attack the lion by trying to jump on its back and strangle it from above. Fired with courage in the face of death, he ran towards Rano.

The lion, its nose almost touching Rano, was just about to spring when it caught sight of Milon. It stopped mid-bound and crouched, turning towards the approaching figure. Milon slowed his step. He drew closer to the great predator, eye to eye. Just then, a loud roar rose from the crowd at the opposite side of the arena. The other lion had overwhelmed Pinaro and torn him apart.

Milon approached the crouching lion step by step, with cool fearlessness. The crowd grew silent; a breathless tension gripped

the arena. Suddenly Milon called to the lion as he had once done by the five olive trees. The animal, about to pounce, raised its nose to sniff the air; then it stood up and broke into a strange yowl. Now the lion, its tail waving, gave a small jump towards Milon in greeting.

"This is *my* lion!" said Milon in shock. "The one I once helped by pulling a thorn from its paw!"

He opened his arms wide and flung them around his old friend's neck. He stroked the lion's mane, tears of joy dampening its fur.

The Romans sat for a moment, frozen at this extraordinary spectacle. As long as there had been an arena in Rome, no such thing had been seen. Soon thunderous applause broke loose, shouts, and exclamations of delight. The lion now crouched on the ground, Milon bent over him, pressing his head against the lion's. The storm of applause turned into a thousand shouts of, "*Vivat! Vivat!* He should live! He should live!"

All eyes turned towards Caesar, who raised his right arm, thumb up. This meant, *Mercy! Free him!* Already a rope was being lowered over a wall for Milon to climb up to freedom.

Then something completely unexpected happened. From the opposite side of the arena the other lion, still hungry for blood, came bounding towards them with a red-flecked mane. It veered towards Milon who, now standing, wondered for a moment if he should leave his lion and take the offered rope. But Milon's lion had noticed the attacker. It let out a low growl and turned fiercely towards the other lion to defend its friend.

Once again the arena thundered with applause. This was unheard of: a lion defending a human being! Many called out, "This slave must be a great magician to have such power over wild animals!"

Caesar ordered that the strange lion tamer be brought to him immediately. Milon's lion had driven off the attacker, who retreated growling.

From the main entrance the circus master waved and called to Milon, "Come, leave the arena!"

He was ready to do that; but his lion must come with him. Then he noticed Rano pressed against the wall in mortal fear. Milon beckoned to him. "Come!"

With one fist gripping its mane, he led the lion, with the other he greeted the Roman people. He walked through the open archway to thunderous applause, and Rano accompanied him unhindered. There was a short discussion at the gate about whether the lion should remain in the arena. But Milon, encouraged by the shouts of the crowd, demanded a chain, in a voice he didn't know he had in him. Quickly a chain was brought, together with a muzzle, which the lion had worn before entering the arena.

Now the circus master strode towards him, bringing the message that he was to appear before Caesar, up in the gallery. Milon demanded, "The lion must come with me!"

The circus master, in an excellent mood now because of his great success, didn't deny the hero of the day his request. They threw a clean robe over Milon and motioned Rano to follow. The circus master lead the way proudly, while an interval was announced. Milon and the lion were led towards Caesar's gallery, accompanied by guards who kept a sharp eye on the lion, walking beside it with drawn swords. Surprisingly they saw that the animal walked beside the slave like a faithful dog.

As the strange group approached Caesar, the circus master announced the lion tamer. He was waved on, and Caesar said, "Bring him before me!"

Some curiously, some fearfully, the royal household gazed at the lion tamer. Milon threw himself onto the marble steps at Caesar's feet, holding the lion's chain tightly.

Caesar said, "Where have you learnt to tame wild animals? Do you do it with your eyes or with magic words?"

Milon rose to his feet and said honestly, "Noble Caesar, I have not learnt to tame wild animals. This lion is my friend. I got to know him when I served as a shepherd in Egypt." And in a few brief words he told them what had happened by the olive trees when he pulled the thorn from the lion's foot. Attentively Caesar and his entourage listened.

As he finished, Caesar asked, "How on earth did you come to the arena? What had you done?"

Milon described what had happened to him in the house of General Andarius. As he finished his story Caesar replied, "You've been with Andarius! He was my comrade-in-arms in our younger days! The ways of the gods are strange and wonderful; they may even choose slaves as their favourites."

For a moment Caesar looked at Milon, with the lion nestled against him, and something gentle stirred in his harsh soul. He asked, "If you have wishes, tell me. The gods favour you at this moment."

Milon shook with happiness. "Noble Caesar, may I go back to Egypt as a free man and take the lion with me to set him free there also?"

Caesar smiled. "It's a modest wish. It is granted! Is that all?"

A thought crossed Milon's mind: *I've asked for the lion's freedom, but my dearest friends are still imprisoned.* So he stammered, "Oh lord, the sun of your mercy confuses me! May I take my Roman friends — the family of Vero the master builder, who was with me down in the vault, and also my friend Rano here — back to Egypt?"

Caesar exchanged a few words with his councillor, then he answered, "So be it! They may go with you to Egypt. Here, take this ring to my old friend General Andarius as a token of my favour and your good luck." Caesar took off one of his golden rings and handed it to Milon.

The whole royal household applauded as Milon said farewell. The procession, with the lion, left the royal stand. Then the circus master gave instructions to the prison warder about Vero's family, the trumpets blew and the games continued.

Journey Into Freedom

That afternoon, before the games ended, a strange cavalcade could be seen leaving the Colosseum: Milon and his friends. The circus master had handed the lion over to Milon with a flourish and now Rano led him on a chain. Milon's Roman friends followed behind him, and his hand was buried in the lion's mane. Only now did they realise they were free, as they strolled unhindered through the city streets.

Father Vero suggested, "Let's go to my friends for a few days, just outside the city gates, before we go on our journey."

In Milon's belt was a paper, signed and sealed by the royal office, granting them free passage on an imperial ship to Egypt, as well as enough money for the journey. There was nothing to spoil the emigrants' good fortune, and old Vero knew that there were many Christians in Egypt who enjoyed greater freedom than in Rome. Milon also carried Caesar's ring in the belt of his tunic.

It was strange to see how naturally the lion accompanied them as a well-behaved companion. Milon had insisted that he be fed before they left the arena. Wherever the procession passed the lion caused a great stir; children and a large crowd followed at a respectful distance. As Milon reached the triumphal Arch of Augustus, which spanned the road in three arches, you would have imagined that a victorious general was passing through with his entourage. The crowd only stopped following when they reached the gates of Rome.

At sunset they arrived at the estate of Vero's friend, who also belonged to the secret community of Christians in Rome. There was a joyful reunion; Vero and his family had returned from the dead. They sat talking together late into the night, deeply thankful for the guiding hand which had led them through these winding paths of life. The former prisoners spent several good days of rest outside Rome.

One evening the brothers, Bartholomeus and Philippus, went back into the city. Following their grandfather's orders, they were heading to the garden of their former villa to dig up treasure that he'd once buried in an urn, beside a stone well, in preparation for just such difficult times. Old Vero told them exactly which paving stone to lift to find the hidden urn, which contained many gold and silver coins. The gates of Rome were closed at night, so they planned to spend the rest of the evening in the city with friends. A half-moon was just enough to light their way.

When they arrived, the brothers were angry at having to climb the walls of their father's house at night, like thieves. They could hear singing coming from the villa, where the senator who had seized the house was celebrating with friends. Silently the brothers went to work. With a short sword they gently loosened and raised the paving stone. There lay the precious urn. They lifted it into a bag and prepared to return.

As they stood before the wall Philippus whispered, "If we were just Romans, we'd enter the house now and kill the senator with our daggers, but as Christians we can't take revenge."

Old Vero welcomed his two brave grandchildren back warmly the next day. The fortune they'd brought would provide for them on the journey to Egypt. Vero didn't for a moment think of returning to his old life. Destiny had spoken and pointed the way to Egypt. So after a week, the travellers said goodbye to Rome.

Milon and his friends were standing on the deck of the ship when at last the coast of Egypt appeared out of the blue sea. All eyes gazed towards the distant strip of land, which stretched like a frail line, a new unknown destiny in the hazy blue.

What will happen this time? Milon thought, his head ringing with questions. *Will Caesar's ring pave my way with Andarius? Will I be able to tell him the truth? How will I face Lesco? Will Baarla be as happy at my return as I will be to see her again? Will I continue to work with Andarius as a free servant? And will the lion get used to the wilderness again after so long in captivity? Or should I keep and tame him?*

As land approached he suddenly wondered whether Vero might built a temple for Christ in Alexandria, as he'd done for Jupiter in Rome. It was as if they'd both had the same thought, because Vero said, "I would like to build again in this new land. My sons want to help me. Are you with me?"

Milon hesitated. "I'm not sure what I'll do in Egypt yet, but it makes me very happy to think that you'll build with your sons. Maybe I can ask General Andarius to advise you, because he knows the Roman governor and noblemen in Alexandria well. I'd like to help on *one* of the buildings — a temple for people who come together in the name of Christ."

Vero started back in amazement. "You've read my very thoughts and deepest wishes! I've been considering what a Christian temple might look like since we were first imprisoned. When I lay on my pallet during sleepless nights, in my thoughts and dreams I was building. This new temple shouldn't be resplendent with proud pillars; it must lead people into stillness, into themselves, where Christ can draw near in holy deeds and prayer. Our small, consecrated chapel in the catacombs must now be lifted and built on the earth. The old altar, which used to hold blood sacrifices for the Roman gods, must now become the table of the Lord." Then Vero was silent, his eyes shining with hope and trust as he looked across to the emerging shores of Egypt.

A gaping crowd always gathered when a large ship arrived in Alexandria, to watch the new arrivals. Amongst the passengers to be marvelled at this time were Milon and the lion. It was not unusual for lions to be shipped in cages to Rome, but a lion returning from Rome on a chain was something new. As the lion padded peacefully across the bridge with the passengers, the onlookers gasped in amazement. The other travellers were besieged by merchants and carters as soon as they stood on the dock; but no one came near to Milon and his companions. He had handed the lion over to Rano to lead, as he'd proved to be a good carer. No one dared approach the animal, even though it wore a muzzle.

Milon accompanied his friends to a guesthouse near the temple of Neptune, not far from the harbour. He asked them to look around the city for a few days, while he took the ring to Andarius. He then ordered a driver with a fast chariot, and he and Rano climbed in with the lion. Soon they were driving, with a crack of the whip, through the city streets like noble Romans, where a few months ago, they'd both dragged their chains as slaves.

We Meet Again in the House of Andarius

When Milon's chariot stopped in Andarius' courtyard, he sent his servant Rano to the villa before stepping out. A dog on a chain barked wildly. The housekeeper opened the gate to see who'd arrived. Rano bowed his greeting and informed him, "There's a visitor from Rome in the courtyard, who brings a message to General Andarius from Caesar."

The housekeeper sprang to life. He opened his eyes wide and threw a searching glance in the direction of the carriage, but he didn't recognise the Roman guest. Quick as a flash he disappeared into the house to tell his master, who was sitting on the terrace with his wife in the shade of the palm trees.

"A message from Caesar in Rome?" said Andarius. "There must be a mistake!"

But he rose quickly and went to the courtyard to question the messenger. Pyrra, quite against the custom of the land, hurried after him so she'd didn't miss this important event.

Meanwhile the carriage had moved a little closer. As Andarius stood on the front steps, he stopped short for a moment. What was that? Was it not Milon, his former slave, standing on the chariot, clothed in a white tunic embroidered with colourful bands, holding the mane of a lion? Andarius stood on the marble steps, as though rooted to the spot, staring wide-eyed and open-mouthed at the carriage. Was someone playing a trick on him, or ...?

A cry from Pyrra brought him back to his senses, and he realised that it was Milon who stood before him, and the lion appeared to be the very same one he'd captured with the Roman soldiers. But what was going on? And he was said to carry "a message from Caesar"!

Now Milon bowed his head and smiled. "Noble general, I bring you a greeting from Caesar in Rome."

With these words the spell on Andarius was lifted. He walked down the marble stairs, boldly took a few steps towards the carriage and asked, "Excuse me, unexpected messenger, if I seem surprised! Please come, enter my house as a guest, but tell me, by all the good gods — is your name not Milon?"

By now, Baarla and a few other curious servants had gathered in the courtyard. The stranger gave the lion's chain to his attendant, swung down from the chariot and replied, "Yes, noble master, I was once your slave, Milon. In Rome Caesar gave me my freedom, thanks to my lion here." He waved to Rano, who handed the lion over to him again.

Andarius could sense that something extraordinary must have happened, a gift of the gods, rarely revealed so clearly. He lifted his hand in Roman greeting, pointed to the terrace and said, "Dear Milon, be my guest! Come and tell me!"

He walked up the marble stairs, followed by Milon and his lion, whose chain he fastened around the trunk of a slender palm tree in the terrace garden. Now Pyrra, who at first had shrunk away in fear of the lion, returned, greeting Milon warmly, as if they were old friends. She offered him a stately chair to sit on and urged Baarla to bring a jug of wine. When Baarla appeared in the archway of the house with downcast eyes, Milon stood up to greet her. But she put the jug down quickly and, before he could speak, went shyly back into the house.

Andarius laughed. "Everything has changed! Look, Milon, we're all equally confused by your strange return. Now, tell us everything that's happened since you were here last."

So Milon began his story. First he described his meeting with the lion by the five olive trees; but this time he didn't omit the removal of the thorn. He also explained why he didn't mention it before: he was afraid that they'd call him a show-off or even a liar.

Andarius found this part of the story so extraordinary that he said, "Milon, if you'd not shown me today, I would have considered it impossible. Yes, I would have looked upon your lion story as an invention, a fantasy. But go on!"

Milon turned to Pyrra. "Honoured lady, now that I'm a free man I can at last explain that I didn't steal your ring. Someone hid it under my mattress maliciously. Lesco couldn't bear that I, the shepherd, should take his place in the house. He took the ring and blamed me, out of envy and to get rid of me, so that he no longer had to work in the field. He hated being a shepherd and hoped to return to house service in my place."

Pyrra listened with growing excitement. "So my feelings didn't deceive me! I couldn't believe that you'd stolen from me, Milon. My heart knew that you were innocent. But everything happened so fast, one blow after another, and in the moment I could only let things take their course."

Andarius' head sank for a moment as he remembered how hard he had punished the supposed thief; that he'd had him whipped and cast out on the slave market with the criminals. But then he urged, "Continue, Milon, how did you get to Rome? What happened there?"

Before continuing the story Milon said thoughtfully, "In Rome I realised that sometimes we're steered through life by a guiding hand, which leads us to an unexpected goal. Since that day at the olive trees, when I found courage to take the thorn from the lion's paw, such a hand has guided my destiny. This same hand led me to Alexandria, sold me to a Roman trader and decided that I would fight with wild animals in the Colosseum. The lion followed the same path to Rome, then recognised and protected me in the arena.

Now Milon told them how he'd met the Christians in prison and found brotherhood with them. As he described his entrance to the arena, how he'd greeted the Roman people as he'd been told to before, probably, being cruelly torn to pieces by beasts, he seemed to relive the moment, and at times his voice trembled and he fell silent.

"As the two lions, roaring, charged in, looking round for a victim, *one* thought gave me courage and strength: that if I had to die my soul would not be lost. Then one lion came towards me, and at first I didn't recognise him. If I was to die I wanted to fight with courage. I faced him eye to eye. With that my tongue clicked and words came to my lips, as they had done once before, when I called to the wounded lion by the olive trees. The lion stopped short, and yowled with joy as he recognised me, and I him. He licked my hands and feet, instead of pouncing on me. Then he protected me from the other lion."

Pyrra had tears in her eyes. Andarius stared across at the lion lying in the shadow of the palm trees. Milon paused in his story as he wondered what to do about the lion. *Should I take the lion to the wilderness and set him free, or keep him with me and tame him fully?*

Andarius brought him back by asking, "What did the Romans in the arena say to your friendly reunion?"

Milon told him how the crowds had roared their applause and called upon Caesar to give him mercy; how he received the order to come before Caesar and how he'd managed to free Rano as well, although their other companion had already died.

Andarius interrupted, "You didn't go before Caesar with the lion?"

"Yes, I asked for a chain and a muzzle. Everyone was so confused by what was happening that I was given everything I asked for, so I took him with me. He behaved so well with me that Caesar thought I was an animal tamer and had a magic eye. I had to explain that I'd met the lion before and where I came from. So I mentioned Egypt and your name, honoured general. Caesar remembered you well. He was full of mercy, and spoke of the guidance of the gods, who had chosen a lowly slave. He granted all my wishes, gave me freedom, and the lion; and here, noble Andarius, this golden ring for you, which I give to you now in his name and with his greetings."

Milon stood up and took the ring from his belt. Andarius was speechless, struggling to find words as he gazed at the jewel. He turned it round and round and eventually put it on his finger. Milon thought he glimpsed a warm glow in Andarius' usually hard eyes as he said, "I thank you for these greetings and the gift. Faithfulness is the most beautiful token of friendship. It was

126

years ago when Caesar and I were brothers-in-arms, campaigning against the enemies of Rome and defending each other's lives. When he became Caesar he gave me his favour. For some years I served far away in the Eastern Empire. Now my name is no longer well known, but true friendship can't be forgotten. This ring of Caesar's will be a joy in my old age!"

Now Andarius rose and walked towards Milon, and the master embraced his former slave. He said solemnly, "Milon, I have no children of my own. If you agree, I would like to welcome you into my house as my son. Let's fulfil what began in the hands of the gods and was inscribed into our common destiny. From now on, be my son!"

Milon was overwhelmed. He took Andarius' hands, searching for words of thanks and consent, but he couldn't find them.

Then Pyrra stepped to his side, took his right hand and said, "Dear Milon, the ring on my hand became your misfortune and your great suffering. In wonderful ways it led you to the ring of Caesar, which has brought us together in happiness. Stay with us from now on, help my husband look after his estate. He needs your help. In all freedom we offer you our friendship. You will be like a son to us."

With these words from Pyrra, Milon no longer doubted that the circle of destiny was complete. He said, "Noble Pyrra, noble Andarius! Forgive me, for I can only find clumsy words to thank you. From my heart, I accept your generous offer to live here again. I'd like to prove myself worthy of your trust and kindness."

He paused for a moment and then went on, "I only have one concern. Perhaps, noble Andarius, you may be able to help me. What should I do with the lion, which lies here so quietly? He's an animal born to freedom. Despite his faithfulness to me, I sense that he's grown more restless since we stepped back onto Egyptian soil. Should I try to tame him and suppress his natural drives? Or should I set him free?"

Andarius looked over at the sleeping animal and replied, "Milon, there's only *one* enduring happiness for a wild animal like your lion, and that's freedom in the wilderness. His affection for you is incredible and unique, but when the southerly wind brings the scent of the wild, his true nature will become clear. In the morning, I'll take you southwest to the edge of the desert. There you may give the lion the freedom that Caesar has given to you!"

Although for himself it would mean a great sacrifice, Milon was now sure he could give no greater gift to his lion than to set him free. He clasped the hand that Andarius offered and said, "Agreed, so be it!"

Laughing, Andarius replied, "Who'd have thought that I'd change from a lion-catcher to a lion-freer. We'll set off early in the morning."

No one was happier with this outcome than Pyrra. She was afraid of this predator, even when it slept peacefully, but she'd have tried to overcome her fear if Milon had chosen to keep the lion. As she contentedly watched her husband and young Milon, she heard the rumble of an approaching wagon in the courtyard.

"That's the steward with Lesco!" she said. "They've been shopping in Alexandria."

The general's face darkened. They had completely forgotten about Lesco in their happiness. "That shameless one! He's brought a dark stain upon my justice with his slander. His punishment will be severe!" Milon pressed his lips together and listened for sounds from the courtyard.

Andarius turned to him. "I'll leave it to you to punish this scoundrel as you like; his life means nothing to me any more. I would have him whipped to death. Now he is yours. Be his harsh judge and avenger!" Andarius descended the terrace steps into the courtyard to speak with the steward. Pyrra went into the house to take care of the evening meal with Baarla.

All the time Rano, the lion's faithful guardian, had sat inconspicuously beside the creature. The lion had woken at the rumble of the wagon. Rano now grasped its chain and asked Milon if he could take the lion for a walk and have food and drink brought out. The hounds in the courtyard had been locked in the barn since the lion's arrival so that there would be no unpleasant encounters.

Milon remained alone on the terrace, a battle surging within him. Once again he saw Lesco's malicious grin as he had boarded the wagon, battered and bloodied, to be taken to the slave market in Alexandria. Once again he lived through his misery and fear in prison. His blood boiled. Then he heard the gentle voice of old Vero, as he spoke of forgiveness and love. No, he couldn't go to the courtyard and meet Lesco with this turmoil in his heart. He didn't know if he'd be able to control himself. As he stood there, undecided, he heard a man scream ... or was it an animal? Milon sprang up. Between the screams he heard the crack of a leather whip. Was Lesco being punished without his order?

He leapt down the steps and across the courtyard. Lesco's arms had been bound around a stone pillar. The supervisor's whip whistled over his naked back. Nearby stood Andarius and the steward in urgent conversation.

Milon stepped towards them, briefly greeted the surprised steward and asked, "Was I not to decide on the punishment?"

"Certainly," replied Andarius, "but when I asked him about the stolen ring, the scoundrel lied to my face once again. Twenty strokes are from me. The rest are for you to order." When the last stoke of the whip fell silent, Lesco hung bleeding and groaning on the pillar.

The steward stepped towards Milon and offered him his hand. "Milon, I congratulate you on the mercy which the gods have granted you. This scoundrel lied to me and I was blinded into thinking you were the thief. Forgive me, and let me too be your faithful servant." Again he offered his hand and bowed in devotion to the new young master, as Andarius had called him. Then the steward left the courtyard with the general. The slave supervisor waited, whip in hand, for Milon's order.

"Untie him!" Milon ordered.

The supervisor had expected to whip his victim to death. Disbelieving, he gaped at his new master. But with a wave of his hand Milon made his order clear. The bonds were loosened.

Lesco still knew nothing of Milon's return, and hadn't understood why the master had asked him about long forgotten things and ordered him to be beaten. Now he braced himself against the pillar and gazed behind him. He saw the supervisor with the whip walk away across the courtyard. But who stood unmoving close behind him? He turned his head a little more. His eyes widened. A shudder ran through his whole body, and a sound jerked from his throat, "Milon?"

His arms slid from the pillar and he collapsed silently on the ground at Milon's feet. Milon, looking down on him, remembered his own pain. He saw the streams of blood that ran into the dust and trickled between the cobblestones. Half questioning, half reprimanding, he replied, "Lesco?!"

With a jerk Lesco turned to clutch Milon's legs and press his forehead on his feet. Milon bent down, lifted him under one shoulder and said, "Lesco, stand up!"

The wounded man straightened up with difficulty, and Milon

led him slowly to the slaves' sleeping quarters. There Lesco sank onto his mattress, face down with his wounded back facing upwards. He lay there motionless, dumb with pain.

"I didn't wish for you to be beaten," Milon said. "I'll send Baarla to tend your wounds."

Milon entered the villa to find Baarla, who was about to lay the table in Lesco's place. Pyrra had told her about his experiences in Rome and his new position in the house. She bowed her head as a slave before Milon as he came towards her. But he said, "Baarla, give me your hands in greeting; I still hope to be your brother, as before, when you cared for me in my misery."

She raised her dark eyes to meet his, filled with gratitude, and offered him her hand, asking, "Did you find Christians in Rome?"

"Yes, Baarla, I'll tell you all about it, and you'll meet old Father Vero soon. He was persecuted as a Christian in Rome, but he and his family came with me to Alexandria. He heard the apostle Paul preaching and was baptised by him. He's full of wisdom and goodness. But listen to me now: Lesco is lying over in the slave quarters with bloody wounds. He was beaten because of me. Go, take care of his wounds, and soothe his pains, as you did with me. He should be forgiven. Wasn't he a necessary tool in guiding my path to Rome? His blame has turned to blessing for me and others."

"I'll go to him immediately. The table's ready. Mucius, the new servant, can continue here." Baarla hurried back to the kitchen. She poured hot water over crushed healing herbs, in the same basin she'd once used for Milon; she took a jug of drinking water and a bowl of grapes. As she crossed the courtyard towards the slave quarters she met the supervisor.

He stopped her. "What are you going to do?"

"I'm following Milon's orders," she answered.

Immediately the supervisor softened and said, "All right! Very good!" and he let her pass.

Baarla entered the dismal, empty upstairs. She noticed Lesco lying on one of the mattresses at the back. He hadn't yet seen

131

her, and he lay there groaning and breathing heavily. When Baarla put the jug down next to him, he shrank away and looked around fearfully.

She said, "Milon has sent me to care for your wounds. Here, have a drink."

Half-crazed, Lesco asked, "What happened? Why is he here? Why did he come back? Who discovered it?"

Baarla answered, "Lesco, this is a good day for you, even though it's a day of pain. Your whole future life of guilt and sin would have remained hidden. Milon returned for the sake of the truth. He was given his freedom in Rome, and he will live in the house of Andarius."

"So the gods have helped him again and thrust me even deeper into ruin. He will forever be taking revenge on me as he's done today by having me whipped."

"No, you're wrong! He will not take revenge. You were whipped without his knowledge because you lied to Andarius. Didn't Milon bring you here, then send me to take care of you? He forgives you and he hopes that you can become a whole person again." As she spoke she gently washed Lesco's wounds and laid healing herbs on them.

When Baarla left him, Lesco sank back into feverish dreams. Whenever he woke for a moment, he heard the words Baarla had spoken: "Become a whole person again ..."

Last Journey with the Lion

Early next day the courtyard seethed with excitement. The servants and slaves had talked until late in the night about Milon's return. Nobody wanted to miss the lion's departure. Every resident of the estate gathered in the courtyard. Milon had asked the steward if they could all attend, and he had given his permission. Already the horses were harnessed to the wagon and impatiently pawing the stone-paved courtyard.

As Andarius and Pyrra appeared from the villa, accompanied by Milon and the lion, something occurred which had never happened in that courtyard before: everyone broke into joyful applause, clapping their hands as if they were in the Roman arena. Master and mistress beamed with joy. Milon waved to his former fellow slaves, greeting them with one hand; with the other, he firmly held the chain on which the lion was visibly tugging, as if he too sensed the importance of the moment.

The driver was already seated. Andarius climbed up, and when Milon followed, the lion, with one jump, leapt up too. Rano was travelling with them, to hold the lion if he became unruly. The horses stamped. The driver gathered up the reins and the vehicle rattled across the courtyard to the entrance. Loud cheers broke out once again, waves and shouts of goodbye followed the disappearing wagon.

Above in the slave quarters two dark eyes bored through a small window, watching the spectacle from a hidden vantage point. Lesco had been given permission to stay off work today to tend his wounds. When he heard the noise in the courtyard, he rose to watch the departure, despite the burning pain in his back. A change had come over him since yesterday.

When he sank down under the whiplashes on the pillar in excruciating pain and Milon had suddenly stepped towards him, lifting him up gently, had he not said softly, "Poor Lesco"? Or had he dreamt in some feverish delusion that Milon had carried him here? Then Baarla had come to care for his wounds. He remembered exactly what she'd said to him: "Milon sent me to take care of you. He forgives you and he hopes that you can become a whole person again." Yes, that's exactly what Baarla had said. He went over these words again and again in his mind. He knew he would never forget them. There was comfort in them, which eased the pain in his soul, in the same way as Baarla's care had soothed the wounds on his back.

Lesco left the window and wandered back to his mattress. In the half-dark he stared at the bare walls. Had Milon found the words to repay evil with good in Rome? And who had taught him? He himself had never heard anything other than: blood for blood, eye for an eye, tooth for a tooth, and revenge for revenge! He must ask Baarla. He could trust her.

Andarius' horses trotted steadily southwards along the dusty roads, guided by their experienced driver. The midday sun was burning hot by the time they reached the hills bordering the desert hours later. Andarius ordered them to stop. The lion's chain rattled as it sprang off the wagon with Milon. Milon poured water for the lion from a large jug, and it lapped it up eagerly. Then the driver, horses and Rano rested in the shade of some thorn trees, while Andarius, Milon and the lion walked towards a small hill.

Freed from its muzzle the lion was restless, stopping now and again to lift its head, its nostrils sniffing the southerly wind. Suddenly a tremble shook its body, and it pulled on the chain. Andarius nodded to Milon who, clenching his teeth, gripped the collar and loosened the leather noose. Collar and chain fell into the desert grass. Once again, as he had in the arena, Milon embraced the mane and chest of his beloved lion. For the last time a wet tongue stroked his hand, and the lion growled softly. Was it a farewell? Was it a greeting to the wide, free lands? Milon loosened his arms from the body of the lion, which narrowed its eyes, lifted its head and sniffed a deep breath of the desert wind.

Then slowly, it stepped forward between the clumps of long, dry grass. When it reached the top of the hill it turned its splendid head in a last glance towards Milon, then its muscles tensed. In great leaps it set off over the bushes towards freedom.

Milon ran a few steps up the hill to watch it, his heart pounding with joy and pain. Tears stung his eyes and he wept as he hadn't done since their meeting in the arena. The lion got smaller and smaller until it disappeared in the distant scrub. Milon stood gazing after him. He closed his eyes and felt a deep sense of gratitude in his heart. He thanked the voice of his destiny, which, here on this hill, spoke to him so overpoweringly now that the lion had gone.

After a while he opened his eyes in the blinding midday sun and found himself alone. Andarius had gone back to the wagon. He didn't want to disturb Milon's farewell. Even as a hard-fought general he felt sad as he witnessed how the lion had turned away from Milon, following his ancient instincts into the desert. But he also knew that he was right to welcome this much-tested young man as a son. With Milon, his own life would gain new meaning. He pondered these thoughts until Milon returned to the wagon, showing nothing of the inner struggle he'd gone through.

With a cheerful voice Milon asked Andarius, "May I drive the horses on the way back, noble father? I'd love to do that!"

"Well, you may, if you promise we won't end up in the Nile with the crocodiles!" replied Andarius. So they climbed into the wagon and the driver handed the reins to Milon who, for the first time, drove a proper team of horses.

Andarius said to Rano, "I notice that a lion tamer has no difficulty in driving horses!"

135

Meeting in Alexandria

Late in the afternoon, after a long journey, they arrived at a fork in the road, left to the estate and right to Alexandria.

Milon drew the reins in and stopped to ask Andarius, "Would it be too tiring for you, father, to take a trip to Alexandria? I'd like to go to the Neptune guesthouse to see my Roman friends, and introduce them to you."

Andarius, who appreciated being called "father" by Milon agreed to go. So Milon drove the horses towards Alexandria, and they soon arrived in the city. As the crowds of people and chariots grew busier Milon handed the reins over to Rano, who as a former driver for a Roman master, knew how to wind his way through a city full of vehicles.

They found the Neptune near the harbour, and Andarius chose to wait outside in the wagon. "It's not proper for a noble Roman to enter a public guesthouse," he said.

Milon found his friends in the courtyard where they were expecting him. What a happy reunion! Vero immediately saw that something in Milon had changed. Had he been disappointed? Had he not been well received by the general?

Abruptly Vero asked, "How's the lion?"

At first Milon was silent. Everyone looked towards him expectantly. "He's very well! He's free and hurrying south towards the desert!"

No one said a word; they all knew how attached Milon had been to his lion.

Suddenly Milon said, "Vero, I nearly forgot! General Andarius, my former master, is outside in front of the guesthouse waiting for me in the wagon. Please come with me to greet him. He's welcomed me as a father and he'd like to meet you too."

Milon took his Roman friends to Andarius, who greeted

them graciously. Then the general fixed his eyes on old Vero and asked, "You were a master builder in Rome? Didn't you extend the northern gates of the city and the fortifications about thirty years ago?"

"Yes, certainly, they were built according to my plans."

"Then we've already met. I was in the defence council of the city at that time, and I had to deal with this matter. I remember you well, only your name had escaped me." Andarius shook Vero's hand once again, happy that he'd found someone who he could talk to about the old days in Rome.

Suddenly he turned to Milon. "How would you like it if your friends were to come and stay with us on the estate, until they find permanent accommodation in Alexandria? Our guesthouse is always empty, and our estate provides plenty to live off."

This offer was received by everyone with surprise and gratitude. Used to commanding, Andarius ordered, "Dear friends, we can't take you all in our wagon now, so I'll send for you tomorrow. Be ready for the journey, and by then our guesthouse will be ready to receive you."

The Vero family all thanked him heartily and the grandfather said, "So it often goes in life, where one gate closes another opens!"

Leaving the city on the return journey, Milon noticed that Andarius was deep in thought. He didn't start conversation, but turned things over in his own mind. How much had changed in a few days! He wouldn't have dared to ask Andarius to accommodate his friends, but their path had been wonderfully smoothed. What a good hand wove the threads of destiny! Although he still mourned for the lost lion, life was giving him other tasks now, which demanded all his strength.

Milon was roused from his thoughts by Andarius, who asked, "Milon, tell me about these Christians. You told me that Vero is one of them. How did Vero, such a respected Roman, come to this new faith?"

So Milon began, "In the prison of the Colosseum and on the long voyage Vero told me many things. He told me how he helped to build the Temple of Jupiter in Rome, although he knew that the old gods had vanished, that their marble statues were empty. The people had become superstitious and the priestly sacrifices were nothing but a show. For some time he waited for a miracle, hoping that a god might move into the newly built temple. The temple was finished in glistening marble, but there was no sense of presence, no spirit of god appeared to enliven the people and work through them. It was nothing but a beautiful showpiece for the city of Rome. Then Vero began to meet people who had no temple, but in whom a god was visibly working and speaking. These people told of the new hidden God who now unites himself with humanity. Vero will gladly tell you about him, once he's settled with us, A strange miracle occurred in Palestine, which I can hardly grasp or put into words."

In between the rattling of wheels and the crack of the whip Milon gave Andarius all these answers and he listened attentively, thinking, *Vero interests me. He has the dignity of a Roman and the refinement of an Athenian. He told me that his father had been a famous sculptor in Greece, who came to Rome and took on a Roman name and Roman customs. But there's still something I question: how can one speak of a new god? Certainly, the old gods have become pale to us, shrunk to mere marble figures. I no longer sacrifice to them. Only my wife takes care of the small house altar, where, superstitiously, she tries to conjure up good spirits.*

Andarius carried on thinking, *It seems that Milon, too, has a leaning towards this new Christian faith. His voice sounded deeper, more fulfilled when he spoke about it. But why does Caesar persecute these Christians? He must have his reasons. And how could such a capable and deserving man as Vero be banned from Rome?*

Andarius resolved to get to know these Christians and their work better; to test and, if necessary, to help shed light on their errors.

Alexandria at Night

As soon as Andarius drove away from the Neptune guesthouse, Philippus and Bartholomeus turned to their father Marius. "Up to now we've stayed at home so we didn't miss Milon. But since he's been, can we look around the city? We'd like to cross the Heptastadion, the long causeway that leads to the Isle of Pharos where the great lighthouse that we saw in the distance stands. You were telling us, Father, that it's named as one of the seven Wonders of the World, built by the Greek, Sostratos."

Dina, their mother, interrupted anxiously, "But this city is wild and dangerous, especially at night. It's so large it would be easy to get lost. Then we'd face another disaster."

Marius understood the youngsters' longing to go exploring and said, "I'd love to see the city myself, but I'll save it for tomorrow. You and I, Dina, and old father can stroll through the city together at a more leisurely pace than our two runners. Perhaps Milon will come with us as well. Just let the two young fellows go. They're clever and skilful enough, and they won't do anything dangerous."

Grandfather Vero, listening to their conversation, encouraged them. "They've been imprisoned for too long. They should get out and see the world. Here, have some money just in case." He handed them each a few silver coins and soon, cheerfully, they were on their way out of the guesthouse.

They entered the main street of the city, called Dromos, and were astonished at its breadth. Even Rome didn't have a street like this. Twenty wagons could have lined up next to each other across that street. The Alexandrians called it *Plateia*, the "wide one".

After their long imprisonment and the narrow confines of the ship, the two brothers strode briskly, weaving to and fro

139

among the crowds. They marvelled at stalls laden with goods from Africa, Arabia and Asia. In one great square, on a carpet on the ground, crouched a snake charmer, displaying his skill. With the beckoning tones of his flute, he lured a snake out of a clay pot. It rose upright, swaying to the music. Close by, a conjurer produced coins by magic and made them disappear before his gaping audience. A woman fortune-teller gathered a ring of customers, and foretold the future from the lines on their palms. A colourful crowd of Africans, Arabs, Jews and Romans moved through the streets and squares. Wagons rumbled in all directions across the paving. Every now and then came the loud swearing of drivers and fierce crack of whips, as two vehicles rammed into each other; crowds gathered round to watch the spectacle.

As the sun dimmed and the merchants in streets and marketplaces began to pack away their wares, there came a sudden cry. A carpet dealer, carrying a bundle of rolled carpets on his shoulders, almost fell to the ground next to Philippus, dropping his load on the stone paving. The two brothers and other passers-by helped the old man to his feet and tried to collect his carpets. Then Philippus saw a stranger grab a rolled-up carpet and slip away with it into the crowd. Philippus was up and after him! In no time his brother Bartholomeus lost sight of him. He hurried after, pushing his way through the crowds.

The dealer who'd been robbed cried out at the top of his voice, "Stop thief! Stop thief!"

Some of the bystanders thought Bartholomeus must be the thief. As he pushed through the crowd, a tall soldier grabbed his clothes and shouted at him, "Stop, wretched scoundrel!"

Bartholomeus tried to break away, but several people pulled him to the ground. By the time he'd explained, and they realised he had no carpet, the real scoundrel and his brother Philippus had long since disappeared.

The fleeing thief was quick and wound snake-like through people and vehicles. Right across the broad street he went, disappearing into a narrow lane. He must have known the area and the buildings well, because he suddenly turned down stone steps into the dark entrance vault of a cellar. Here he ducked in a corner. His pursuer, close on his heels, saw him turn, and was about to descend the steps when the thief leapt out from his hiding place, hurtling past Philippus, and fled. Philippus fell down the steps, struck his head against the cellar door and lay unconscious at the bottom in the dark.

Bartholomeus wandered around looking for his lost brother. At last he returned to the dealer who still hoped in vain that someone would return his stolen carpet. Bartholomeus thought, *Surely he'll come back here, with or without the carpet.*

An hour passed. It grew dark. The streets and squares emptied. Philippus didn't appear. The dealer, after asking the name of the guesthouse where the brothers were staying, said goodbye. Bartholomeus waited a while longer, then he called for a torch-bearer who led him back through the dark streets of Alexandria to the guesthouse where he hoped to find his brother. But Philippus wasn't there.

Now the parents were overcome with shock and fear. Marius blamed himself for not having gone with his sons to the city. While old Vero spoke words of comfort, "Don't lose heart; Philippus has always had a good, brave spirit. He will return again, I'm sure!"

So they waited.

But what was happening to Philippus at the cellar door? He hadn't lain there long before footsteps shuffled down the stairs. An old man came by, carrying a lamp to light the way so he didn't miss a step. Suddenly, what was that? His foot touched something soft and he let out a muffled cry. He lowered his lamp and saw the figure of a young man lying there, unmoving. He held the lamp closer to the half-turned face, and saw that blood had stained the stone step. The injured man seemed to be breathing with difficulty. "What's a Roman doing here? Did he get drunk and fall?" he mumbled. Somewhat disturbed he climbed the stairs to fetch help. He crossed the courtyard and disappeared into a high entrance, returning a little while later with two slaves, who carried a second lamp and a bowl of water.

The old man slid back the bolt of the cellar door and told his two helpers, "Lay him on the bench inside; it will be easier to care for him."

Setting down their lamps, the slaves lifted the unconscious man and carried him into the cellar. The old man had hardly poured water over his forehead and washed his face before Philippus opened his eyes. He stared around in wonder when he saw the glimmer of light, the cellar vault above, and the dark, unknown figures. Slowly he lowered one leg from the bench and tried to sit upright.

The old man held him back. "Lie quiet! You've fallen. What happened to you? Who are you?"

Confused, Philippus asked, "Where's the thief? Where am I?"

"We found you here in front of our cellar door. What's your name?" the old man replied.

"I'm Philippus. Is my brother Bartholomeus not here?"

The face of the old man brightened. "Philippus, Bartholomeus! These are the names of the Lord's disciples. Are you a Christian, Roman?"

"*Salve in nomine Christi* — I greet you in the name of Christ!" Philippus murmured. This was the brotherly greeting used by the Christians in Rome.

The lamp in the old man's hand flickered and shook. He called to the slave, "Go quickly, and call my wife!" Then taking the hand of the young man and pressing it warmly, he said, "Philippus, can you tell me what happened to you?"

He told him about his chase after the carpet thief, and that he'd lost his brother, and that they were staying, for a short time, with their parents in the Neptune guesthouse.

"Strange and wonderful!" the old man exclaimed.

"Do you know, young man, *where* you find yourself now? You've tumbled in front of a special door. There are three small communities of Christians in Alexandria. Our Christian gatherings are held in this vaulted cellar, hence the benches and stone seats. We'll be meeting this evening, which is why I came

142

to open the door and to light a candle, and I found you. Soon the first brothers and sisters will be here."

Philippus let his eyes wander round the dimly lit vault. In the centre stood a stone table. He asked, "I wonder how long I lay here. Is it late at night? It was sunset when I chased the carpet thief."

"Mmm, probably less than an hour's passed. It's been dark outside for a little while."

Worried, Philippus asked, "How can I find my way back to the Neptune? My parents and brother will be worried about me. I must go to them!"

With these words he tried to rise again, but the old man shook his head and pressed him gently back. "You shouldn't jump around straight after that heavy fall! It's great luck that you have no broken bones, but it could be serious if you were to get up so quickly. I'll send one of my slaves to the Neptunus with a message for your parents," the old man suggested, and Philippus gratefully agreed.

Just then the old man's wife arrived with another slave. She greeted Philippus and said, "Bring him over to the wooden bench by the wall. He'll be more comfortable there. Here, I've brought some cushions where he can lie quietly."

Philippus let himself be helped across to the bench by the wall. A piercing pain hammered through his head as he moved and lay down again on the carefully arranged cushions. Now the old man sent the youngest of the slaves to the Neptune guesthouse, with instructions to bring Bartholomeus. He offered Philippus a bed upstairs in his house, and for his brother too, if he wanted to stay.

Meanwhile one of the slaves hung lamps on the steps outside and in the cellar vault. The first Christians came. Philippus watched with wondering eyes as a man in a white robe lit three candles on the stone altar and placed a jug and a bowl with bread next to them. A festive silence filled the room, only broken by footsteps on the stairs. Gradually the members gathered in the cellar and took their places on the simple stone benches. They sat in silent expectation. Scented smoke rose from a bowl of smouldering incense.

By now the messenger had arrived at the Neptunus. He asked at the door, "Is Bartholomeus known here?" Quickly he was led to the courtyard where Vero's family gathered by a fire, waiting anxiously for Philippus.

"A messenger for Bartholomeus!" called the host at the courtyard gate and ushered the messenger through with his burning torch. Immediately the frightened family came to life. Everyone rose to meet the torch-bearer.

"I bring a message from Philippus. He lies injured in my master's house, the merchant Jonea. He sends a message that you shouldn't worry. The young man is in good hands for tonight."

The messenger was bombarded with questions. He sat down and told the story as far as he knew it. When he told them that Philippus had met a community of Christians, they spoke with one voice, "Good messenger, lead us to him! We'll all come with you to Philippus!"

It wasn't too far, so they agreed to follow the torch-bearer on foot, and soon they were moving through the streets and alleyways of the dark city. When they arrived at the courtyard the messenger pointed to the lighted cellar steps. "The service has started, but you may go in. People often come late if they've been delayed on the way."

Bartholomeus followed the torch-bearer down the steps, with the others close behind him. They eased open the heavy cellar door with barely a creak and entered into a mood of devotion. The priest was speaking of the Logos, Christ as the light of the world; how, over the course of time, this light had been coming closer and closer towards humanity. How he had entered the darkness of the earth and lived in a human body. Then the priest spoke of the light that burns in all our hearts, which is kindled by the light of Christ; that it must always be protected from the rough winds that try to extinguish this tender flame.

The messenger led the Vero family to the stone bench at the back wall where Philippus lay. They greeted him silently. Dina sat by his head and laid her hand on his shoulder. The others stood at the back wall, listening to the service.

After a prayer the priest walked round the altar, accompanied by some of the congregation. Vero counted twelve. With arms raised in prayer they circled the altar blessing the bread and wine, which lay there covered by a white linen cloth. After some circling they stood still. The priest lifted the cloth and, with his helper, handed bread and wine to those who approached. Father Vero and his family were the last to come. Bartholomeus and Marius supported Philippus, who was determined to join them. A song of thanksgiving began, half spoken, half sung. The family moved back again. A ring of young girls began to dance round the altar carrying burning oil lamps. Then the song faded into silence, and the members of the community began to bid each other farewell.

The Veros were greeted and especially honoured. The news had spread that they were Roman Christians. When they heard that old Father Vero had been baptised by the apostle Paul himself, they asked if he would speak at the next community evening in three days. They wanted to hear all about his meeting with the apostle; of how he had worked and preached and had suffered a martyr's death.

The owner of the house and courtyard who had found Philippus on the steps came to introduce himself. "My name is Jonea," he said. "I've already made friends with Philippus, after his violent fall in front of my door. I'm happy to have him in my house tonight, so he can recover in peace." The family thanked Jonea for his kindness. "Please, come up to my house for a while," Jonea added, "so you can see that Philippus isn't going to be carried to a robber's den!"

Philippus rested on a couch in the hospitable merchant's house. Father Vero asked about Jonea's business and he told them, "For half my life I traded in bales of cloth and carpets, across the sea to Rome and other harbours of the empire. The richer I became the less satisfied I grew and the emptier my soul. The old gods and temples no longer spoke to me. One day a cloth merchant from Jerusalem came to Alexandria as my guest. I noticed something about him that astonished me and which I'd never experienced before: he was thoroughly honest when selling his wares. One evening when we sat together in this room, instead of discussing the qualities and prices of textiles, we began to talk about humanity and the riddles of the world. He spoke about past and future times like a wise man. He told me about a man in whom God's son had lived. His father had met this wonderful person, and had followed him for days at a time to hear him speak about the realm of God and about past and future times on earth. Through his father, he joined the community of Christians in Jerusalem.

"On the following day he introduced me to the Christians in Alexandria. Suddenly, these people became more important to me than my cloth business. After a few weeks the dealer returned to Jerusalem. In the meantime I'd become a Christian too. The community in Alexandria was growing fast. I offered my large cellar for the service, which will soon be too small, as you saw this evening. You're a master builder, Vero, couldn't you build a gathering place for the Christians in Alexandria?"

At this abrupt question Vero smiled at his son Marius and, turning to his host, he said, "Jonea, do you read thoughts? My son can tell you that, as we arrived at the port of Alexandria, I said to him, 'Here in Egypt, I would like to build again ... a temple for the new God, Christ in Jesus!' And when I saw the great beacon at the port, the 'wonder of the world', I said to Dina, 'There's a real wonder in the world — the hidden light that shines wider than any beacon, from land to land, from continent to continent. This is the fire that was kindled in the disciples at Whitsun. I saw it blazing in Paul. This fire is a beacon for souls who search for direction on the waves of life. I want to build an altar and a temple to this hidden fire!'"

Vero fell silent, almost shocked at his own enthusiasm, but Jonea cried, "Vero, you're the man I've been searching for all these years. Here, in the middle of Alexandria, are my great trading yard and many houses. I've been planning to give up the business that has made me rich. Before I grow too old or die, I have a dream: to build a worthy house of God for the Christians in Alexandria. You're the master builder, Vero! With your family's help you could fulfil my dream!"

Jonea stepped towards the Roman architect, holding out his hands. Vero rose and gripped them strongly in answer. "Noble Jonea, I accept your commission. Now I know why I'm in Egypt! When I was down in the cellar watching the celebration around the altar, I had the thought, 'The house of God needs to be round, with an altar in the centre, surrounded by twelve stone pillars, like the twelve disciples of the Lord. Above this sacred centre the roof will be domed, as the vault of the heavens ...'"

Vero spoke with such fervour, as if the building was already standing before his eyes. But it was getting late and Marius reminded him, "Father, it's late. Let's continue building when it's day! Philippus, you can dream tonight of the stars that you'll put in the domed roof, with the colourful mosaic art you learnt in Rome. Bartholomeus knows how to use a chisel and can carve an altar out of stone. I'm used to tussling with building slaves to make sure the stone blocks are well set. But now, the host of the Neptunus shouldn't have to wait for us any longer!"

The Veros and Jonea bid each other farewell. Old Vero added, "I'd love to start work on the building tomorrow, but we've been invited to stay on a nearby estate. In the meantime, I'll think about the plans."

"As soon as you're ready to build," said Jonea, "I'll give you a home in one of my houses. My slaves can help with the heavy work instead of dragging around bales of cloth, and I'm sure many brothers and sisters of our community would like to help too. I look forward to my courtyard becoming a busy building site!"

Jonea sent for a torch-bearer and two armed attendants to guide his friends safely through the streets of Alexandria. As they made their way through the darkness, the Pharos lighthouse suddenly blazed before them, and Vero thought, *Soon we'll be building a house for the inner light of the earth, here in Alexandria.*

Milon Collects his Guests

Next day, in good time, Rano harnessed the horses to a large wagon, ready to bring their friends from Alexandria to Andarius' estate. Milon had no idea of the adventures they'd had the previous evening. Pyrra was delighted to host Roman citizens in her guesthouse. She looked forward to enjoyable days and interesting conversations. Under her and Baarla's direction, the slaves had made the guesthouse clean and welcoming, decorating the rooms with flowers. The building was opposite the villa, on the other side of the garden, and the two buildings were connected by a long colonnade. The garden was laid out gracefully between stone paths and a pool with lotus flowers, all looked after by an old gardener. While the slaves prepared the guesthouse and kitchen, Milon's wagon rolled on its way to Alexandria and the Neptunus. Then there was a cheerful reunion and Milon heard all about the previous evening, about Philippus and the gathering of Christians at Jonea's house.

When Vero told Milon that he'd been asked to build a temple for the community of Christians, Milon exclaimed, "Good friends, Egypt couldn't have received you more wonderfully! Now you'll no longer grieve for the loss of Rome, but build a new home in Alexandria!"

Milon only regretted one thing: that his friends wouldn't stay with him long. They'd soon return to live in the city and start building.

Their luggage was loaded onto the wagon, and the host was paid. The wagon rolled through the city to Jonea's house, to fetch Philippus. As they drew into the wide courtyard of the rich merchant's home, Jonea came out with Philippus and greeted the Veros as old friends. Milon was introduced and Jonea spoke warmly, "You are heartily welcome, Milon. Philippus has already told me about your courage and friendship in Rome. We'd be very happy if you would join our community. It takes a lot of strength to save the lamb of Christ from the Roman she-wolf. Father Vero has probably told you about our plans to build a home for the 'good shepherd' in this courtyard."

Then Vero intervened, "Before we go, I'd like to pace the length and breadth of the courtyard once more, so that while I'm away I can work out a plan. Every day is precious to me now, so I can complete the most beautiful work of my life." He began to stride across the courtyard with careful steps. Jonea brought out a small wax tablet on which he could scribe the measurements with a stylus.

In the meantime Philippus and Bartholomeus took Milon down to the cellar to show him where the service had been held. Philippus stopped at the oak door and touched the wound on his forehead, saying, "Oak wood is almost as hard as my skull!"

Milon stood in the shadowed vault. He pictured himself taking part in the next gathering and promised that he'd bring Baarla with him.

On their return, the measuring completed, Vero clutched the tablet to his chest like a precious jewel. As soon as they were settled in the wagon his son Marius teased him, "Take care, father, the wax is melting on your warm heart, and you'll have to measure all over again!"

Startled, Vero pulled the tablet away to check the surface, while the others laughed merrily and he assured himself that the numbers were unharmed.

Rano drove Milon and the Veros out of Alexandria. Jonea had thrown soft cushions into the heavily-laden wagon for Dina, while the others sat on sacks and leather stools. The conversation was lively, despite the rattle of wheels on cobbles. When the midday sun burned hotter, the horses trotted more slowly and the travellers fell silent. Father Vero nodded sleepily; the wax tablet had fallen from his hand and Marius wrapped it carefully in a white cloth, laying it between the bags in the shade.

Towards evening they arrived at Andarius' courtyard, and

were welcomed by the loud barking of dogs. Servants had set up flaming torches at the entrance, and Andarius and Pyrra came out to greet them. Their belongings were carried to the guesthouse, then master and mistress led their guests to the feasting table.

Eavesdropping

The Roman meal was rich. Afterwards they strolled on the torch-lit terrace. Milon invited Baarla, "Come and sit with us!"

She answered shyly, "It's not fitting for a slave to sit with the master and mistress as equals. I still have something to see to in the guesthouse." She slipped away into the garden.

Milon took Andarius aside and asked, "Good father, would you allow Baarla to sit with us and talk to the guests? You know that we're friends. May she join us as a free person?"

Andarius smiled and said, "It hasn't escaped my attention, Milon, that you love Baarla. You are her master and you may give her freedom whenever you wish."

Milon seized his right hand warmly and was soon hurrying down the terrace steps through the garden to the guesthouse. He slowed when he found Baarla inside, busy lighting oil lamps to guide the guests to bed. She was standing on an armchair as he walked in, fitting a burning light into the ring of a hanging chain. Milon watched from the darkness as she handled the little oil lamp with care. He had loved her since the time she looked after him so kindly, and he wanted to open his heart to her now.

Just then, she stepped down from the chair to reach for another burning light, and she heard her name being called. Startled, she dropped the lamp, which broke on the stone floor.

"Oh, forgive me, Baarla!" Milon apologised. "I've come to take you to join our guests. Andarius has allowed me to bring you, as a free woman, into our circle."

Milon and Baarla walked hand in hand through the dark garden. A half-moon joined the light of the stars. In one hand Milon carried the shards of the broken lamp. When they came to the pool with the lotus flowers he dropped them into the shimmering water and whispered, "Baarla, these shards will rest on the bottom of the pool now, in memory of this night, but our love will never break."

Milon introduced Baarla to the astonished Roman guests as his bride to be. Pyrra laid a gentle arm round Baarla's shoulder and kissed her like a mother. She showed no surprise; she'd seen that they were fond of each other. For a long while Baarla had been no ordinary slave to her, and she'd treated her more as a daughter who loved and served her.

Andarius wouldn't let this news pass without celebrating and he announced to the guests that they'd come to an engagement party. Soon Roman songs sounded from the terrace, struck up by the brothers Bartholomeus and Philippus.

Over in the slave house, a dark head emerged through the small window in the sleeping quarters. Lesco had been woken by the sound of singing, and now he listened into the night. Was it Milon who sang so beautifully? No, there were two other voices leading those joyful songs. As he listened, Lesco felt abandoned and worthless. He stifled the tears that rose in him. Biting with bared teeth on one of the bricks that poked into the window, he breathed heavily.

His thoughts churned. Yes, he'd tried to force his luck with deceit and villainy, and now he was branded with shame and disgrace. He was despised by the master and mistress as well as his fellow slaves. But Milon was good to him; he, the one who he'd brought such misfortune. He would do anything for Milon now, even if he ordered him to jump into the jaws of a wild animal!

The songs had quietened. Only the occasional cheer sounded up from the terrace. *If only I could see those happy people! I'd be able to bear my miserable existence a little better,* thought Lesco.

Suddenly an idea came to him: he could try to step out through the window. One roof was joined to another and by crawling across he could see the garden of the villa. The dogs wouldn't notice him up there. He drew his head back inside and listened to the pitch-dark room. Nothing stirred. He squeezed nimbly through the opening and stepped out onto the roof, which, built in Roman fashion, was fairly flat. What would happen if he was discovered? Half crouching, he moved carefully across the tiles in the direction of the terrace gardens. The singing and cheerful laughter had stopped. Edging nearer, Lesco heard the sound of conversation.

Suddenly a dog bayed. Lesco shrank down in fear, lying flat on the roof. The barking stopped. Perhaps it had been directed at the moon, which they say wakes dogs from their dreams. For a moment Lesco thought of ending his adventure and returning to bed when, from the terrace, he heard a question from Andarius: "Vero, tell me about these Christians in Rome? Why are they persecuted? Are they dreamers, or enemies of Caesar? Is it a mistake that they're seen as dangerous?"

Lesco crept closer, listening intently to hear Vero's answer. Unnoticed in the dark, he peered over the edge of the roof, down onto the gathered company.

There was a short silence after Andarius' question. All eyes were turned towards the master builder, Vero, who began thoughtfully, "Honoured Pyrra and Andarius! You know how Rome, over the centuries, has grown greater and mightier; but its soul has grown harder and darker. I'll try to explain. Early in the morning the sun rises far in the east over Roman lands and sets in the evening far in the west, behind the furthest provinces, into the sea. The sun ripens the daily bread for all mankind; it was created by God and gives life on earth. Since earliest times, when mankind began to sacrifice and give thanks to the gods, they knew that the gods lived and worked in this outer light. So long as people knew that they were embraced by the loving light of the gods, there was a 'Golden Age' on earth, as the Greeks called it.

"But now the fires on the sacrificial altars have been extinguished. The temples of the Golden Age have fallen into decay. Since then, cities, kings and Caesars have built temples like empty marble coffins, for their own glory and honour. Prayers to the true light, the heavenly fire, have grown silent. Evil, lies, hatred and selfishness have found homes in the darkness of human souls. People have forgotten that gods once worked to provide our daily bread. Greed for earthly treasures has gripped them like an illness. People have separated themselves from the realms of heaven and become entirely citizens of the earth." As Vero spoke his voice grew more solemn.

Andarius said, "Good Vero, I completely agree with what you're saying. I've been thinking similar thoughts, too, in my quiet hours. But to see that, I needed no Christianity, no new religion. To me the earth and humanity could be compared to a burning fire that consumes more and more fuel. Eventually it will grow smaller, glow in the ashes and then it will die. All the nations of the earth will gradually burn out and perish. Rome has flickered again, but it will eventually fall under in rubble, dust and ashes to nothing, along with the rest of the world."

Up on the roof, Lesco propped his chin on his hand and listened. His looked down on Vero, waiting for a reply. Everyone on the terrace listened, gripped by what the two elders were saying.

Vero took his turn. "Respected Andarius, your 'end of the world in rubble, dust and ashes' would be a reality if our Creator let everything drift into decline. But it will be different, and this may only be known by Christians up to now. Over in Palestine, a great miracle occurred, so unique that I hardly dare express it in simple words. It's now little more than fifty years since Christ, the son of God, came to live in a holy person named Jesus. The light of the world was with him, and through him this inner light connected with the earth. With him, the realm of God drew closer to humanity. Where he walked, there were miracles: he healed the sick, drove out evil spirits and paved new paths between people so that humanity could know perfect love."

Pyrra, listening almost breathlessly to what Vero was saying, asked, "What do you mean by 'perfect love'?"

Vero answered, "True love can transform evil into good. Love is kind, not jealous or arrogant. It doesn't look for its own benefit or take pleasure in injustice; it only enjoys the truth. Once this spirit of love reaches into people more deeply, a better age can begin on earth, the age of perfect love. This is the message that the apostle Paul shared with us in Rome."

Andarius asked, "Paul? Who's he? I've never heard of him. Is he a Roman?"

"No, he was Hebrew. His former name was Saul. He persecuted the first Christians in Palestine until, outside the city of Damascus, Christ appeared to him in spirit, risen from the dead. From then on he was deeply moved by Christ, and the persecutor Saul became Paul, Christ's apostle. Paul allowed me to become his brother in Rome and I know that his testimony is true. After the burning of the great city, the Caesar Nero wrongly accused the Christians and they were cruelly persecuted. Paul died by the sword, and his blood soaked into the earth of Rome."

When Vero said Nero's name, Andarius' face darkened. He had served Nero in his younger days, and had been disgraced. Only after Nero's death had he been reinstated into the Roman army. "Nero, the dark Caesar, always fought against the light," he said. "It speaks well of the Christians that Nero persecuted them. But why are you persecuted by the present Caesar Domitian?"

Vero told him how a senator, a favourite of Caesar's, had taken his family home and had them all imprisoned.

At that Andarius exclaimed, "So even Caesar Domitian has fallen under the despotism of power! Oh Rome, Rome, where are you going?"

Then, suddenly, everyone turned in surprise, as a tile on the edge of the roof broke and fell to the ground with a loud crash. Although no one was hurt, splinters flew all over the terrace. Everyone except the two elders sprang to their feet, staring startled into the night.

No less shocked was Lesco who, while trying to slide over a loose tile, had clipped it and knocked it to the ground. He quickly threw himself down on the long roof like a cat, where no one could see him. Soundlessly, he crept back to the window, slipped into the sleeping quarters and onto his mattress. He stayed awake till well past midnight, wondering about their mysterious conversation. Up to now he'd only lived from day to day and had given no thought to the world or humanity.

Now that he'd heard how people look for meaning in the riddles of life, one wish filled his heart: *If only I could listen again to the Romans' conversation!*

In the meantime Milon had gathered up some pieces of tile and shown them to Andarius. The general laughed. "A tile, fallen from the roof, nothing else. It can be replaced tomorrow. The wild thunderstorm a few days ago must have loosened it."

Pyrra, always a superstitious soul, whispered to Dina, "Rome will be ruined! The great empire will shatter like a tile!"

She didn't dare to say it aloud. Andarius would have laughed at her. He said cheerfully, "Broken pieces are a good sign! They promised a lucky beginning to Milon and Baarla in their engagement and now they remind us that night calls us to sleep. Thank you, my dear guests, for the rich learning of this evening. My old head is full of new thoughts. I hope my skull won't shatter like the tile!"

Everyone laughed and they bid each other good night. Soon, peacefully, one after another, the lamps shining over the courtyard went out.

But in one of the guest rooms a small light continued to glow long into the night. Propped upright on his bed, Vero worked on a large wax tablet, which he'd requested from Andarius. Now and then he scratched lines and figures into the wax and paused to calculate, then wrote down his measurements. It was the ground plan of a small Christian temple for Alexandria. He had drawn the altar in the middle in the form of a cross, pointing in four directions. Around the altar, at a short distance, stood a circle of twelve pillars. It would all be spanned by a domed roof, which would represent the starry sky. He wanted to show Christ, not only as the god of one nation or land, but as the divine son of the whole universe, become man. But how to construct this domed roof? This caused father Vero many sleepless hours. He'd never built anything like this.

When he eventually fell asleep, the light in his lamp continued to burn. Only when the sun rose did Vero notice how the friendly oil lamp, burning next to his bed, had watched over him through the night, and now merged with the morning light that entered through a narrow window.

He thought, *Fire is an emblem of the eternal light and love that will come to fill the whole world warmly one day. In the new temple a flame should burn day and night, an eternal light, as a token of true Christian love.*

Vero couldn't stay in bed any longer. He wanted to show his night's work to Marius, who would help him with the problem of the domed roof.

We Are Building

"Baarla," Milon asked, some days later, "can you advise me? Andarius is allowing me to send two or three reliable slaves to help with the building, because I can't be there all the time. Andarius is handing more and more of the running of the estate over to me, and I don't want to disappoint him. Who shall I send?"

"Lesco," said Baarla unexpectedly, "He's so keen to serve you I'm sure he would work eagerly for you in Alexandria. I would never have thought anyone could change for the good so quickly, as I've seen in Lesco. He springs up and does the work of two men, and his envy and selfishness are long gone. I think the seed that you planted in him, Milon, with your kindness and forgiveness, has grown. Look, there he is hurrying across the courtyard!"

Milon called Lesco and beckoned to him. "You're in a hurry. What are you going to do?"

"The supervisor has given me orders to wash the chariot and grease the axles to make it run more smoothly. He said you might take part in a chariot race in Alexandria, since Andarius has bought these wonderfully fast horses for you."

Milon smiled. "There's still a while before the chariot races, but I'm glad to own a fast chariot because I travel so often to Alexandria now."

Baarla added, "Well, you could leave the greasing of the axles for now, Lesco. Milon drives far too fast anyway! I'm always afraid when I see him dashing off."

Milon winked at Lesco and continued, "Lesco, I want to ask you: you've heard that the Vero family are going to build a Christian temple in Alexandria. Would you like to join them with two or three others from the estate?"

"To build with the Veros! That would be a great privilege. I couldn't think of anything more wonderful! But I — I'm not worthy to help build a temple; too much shame and guilt weighs upon me. Milon, you shouldn't ask me, but instead command me. If you commanded me to take apart a pyramid of the Pharaohs, I would do it stone by stone!"

Milon and Baarla laughed at this suggestion. "Seriously then, I order you to be ready to travel tomorrow. Choose two of the strong ploughmen who can carry beams and heavy stones, and bring them too. I'll drive you on four wheels to Alexandria."

A gleam of happiness lit up Lesco's face. He felt that Milon wished him well, which filled him with joy. And working with the Veros, he would hear more conversations like he'd heard from the roof that night.

As he turned away he asked, "Shall I oil the four-wheeled wagon too?"

"Yes, do. The faster to Alexandria, the faster I'll be back!"

The following day, Milon, Lesco and two helpers drove to Alexandria. As they approached Jonea's courtyard they saw that the first foundations had already been laid. Here and there the wall stood as high as a man. During the coming days Milon often stayed with Jonea and worked with them. He sometimes took the wagon to fetch building blocks from the brick ovens outside the city. In between he returned to Andarius and helped run the estate. He hadn't brought Andarius to visit the building site yet. He wanted to wait until the building looked more finished.

Weeks passed. The builders made steady progress. The walls were now three times the height of a man and inside the pillars rose higher. The first sign of the roof vaulted upwards above a temporary scaffold of beams.

Then, one day, Milon arrived with Andarius. As they entered the courtyard old Vero saw them and hurried towards them, delighted to see Andarius' astonished expression as he marvelled at how fast the building had progressed.

Milon, who hadn't been there for some time, said laughingly

to Vero, "Every time I return the number of builders has grown. It's like an anthill! Freemen, slaves, brown skinned and black, they're all here to help. Even old Jonea is hammering away at the entrance, if I'm not much mistaken!"

"Yes, he is," agreed Vero. "We couldn't stop him seizing the hammer and chisel to work under Bartholomeus' guiding eye at the entrance. Bartholomeus is inside, working on the altar stone. Look, the pillars are all upright and will soon be able to hold the roof."

Suddenly a greeting rang down from the high walls to Milon. It was Lesco. Milon waved back to him and, beaming with happiness, the young man turned to work on the stone slabs, which they were starting to mortar together for the roof.

Milon asked Vero, "How's Lesco doing?"

"I have to give him credit. He works untiringly. Even during the midday heat, when everyone else is resting in the shade, we can hardly persuade him to come down from the building. He often drags stones, which are hard enough for two to carry, on his own. Only our Christian brothers and sisters have such enthusiasm for the building, as you can see. But only Lesco has such incredible endurance. The fellow is a riddle to me."

Milon was glad to hear this praise, and replied, "To me he is no riddle. Lesco's become a completely changed and happy person since he's been allowed to help with the building. I've heard him singing and laughing at his work. Once, when he thought no one was looking, he danced about on the scaffolding, and I was afraid he would fall! I'm sure he wants to make amends for his mistakes. He feels respected here, and that he belongs to our brotherhood more and more. He's found dignity again through building."

When they reached the temple's entrance, where Jonea had almost finished chiselling, he greeted the guests, laid his hammer and chisel aside and stepped with them into the circle of walls. Milon marvelled at the upright pillars. Beside the stone block of the altar he saw Bartholomeus, so involved in his carving that he didn't notice them entering. On the front of the altar, facing the entrance, a human face was beginning to emerge under his skilful hands.

After greeting him Milon asked, "What are you carving into the sides of the altar?"

Bartholomeus gestured to old Vero and said, "Tell him, Grandfather, it's your idea."

Vero explained, "We stand here on Egyptian soil, where for millennia the secret of the sphinx was guarded: a being partly bull, partly lion, eagle and man. These three animals and the human being, created in the image of God, will be carved on the four sides of the altar. The bull, as an image of earthly power and strength; the lion, as the fiery courage of the heart; the eagle, as the high-flyer, the winged power of thought that strives towards the spirit. They all serve the human being. They are within us, and as images on the altar, they'll carry the offering of bread and wine."

Milon turned towards Bartholomeus. "Dear friend, may I ask you one thing? When you begin on the head of the lion, please let me be your helper! You know who I'm thinking of. May I practise on an ordinary stone today? I can always see the face of my lion clearly before me; I think I'd be able to carve it in stone."

Bartholomeus gave him a discarded stone block, a hammer and a chisel. After sketching a few lines, he said, "So, now, set to work and see if it becomes a lion!"

As Milon began to hammer industriously, Andarius said to Vero, "Now he's glued to a chisel too. All we need is a stone for me to beat!"

"Come, Andarius, I'll take you to Philippus. He's working on his beautiful mosaics. They left the building. Philippus was in the basement of a neighbouring warehouse, which had once been used to store bales of cloth. He was preparing colourful stones and glass cubes, which would later be joined into a great mosaic in the dome. The stones were mostly bluish, intermingled with gilded stars.

"Where do the golden stones come from?" asked Andarius.

Philippus took him to one side, where silk-fine sheets of

hammered gold lay on a small anvil. He took a small, flat stone, spread a resin-like glue over it and pressed the sticky side onto the wafer-thin gold. When he lifted it the stone was gilded.

Andarius asked, "May I try one?"

Philippus encouraged him, and Andarius began gilding pebbles. The gold plating was soon finished, so Andarius tried using one of his gold coins with the head of Caesar, hammering it until it was fine. With some difficulty he succeeded.

In the meantime Vero had left, unnoticed. The thought that even a Roman general was working on the house of God made him very happy.

In the building he found Milon covered in sweat, chiselling away at his lion's head. Marius came in with four workers carrying a ladder, which they set up on the high scaffolding. They carried up bent wooden beams, which would provide a temporary frame for the vaulted roof. While Milon rested for a moment, Marius explained that the roof was calculated on the principle of Roman bridge arches, so that it could be self-supporting, made out of fitted stone blocks.

As Milon was about to start work again, he noticed that Andarius had disappeared. Hurrying outside he met Vero. "Where's Andarius? Is he annoyed with me? Perhaps he's returned home alone?"

Vero grinned, pointing to the mosaic workshop. "Go through that gate, there you'll find the general. He's commanding little stones!"

When Milon went into Philippus' workshop he was delighted to see Andarius, who was busy gilding. Andarius called out cheerfully to him, pointing to a great piece of finely hammered gold, "See, even a Roman emperor can become fine when he is hammered and beaten sufficiently."

Milon laughed. "Father, if you're busy here, I'll return to my lion for a while," and off he went.

Andarius had covered enough stones for Philippus to set them together in a golden star, so he wiped the sweat from his forehead and said, "Now, I'll head back to earth!"

He looked at the golden star, satisfied, and allowed Philippus to praise him for his precise work. He found Milon in the building, standing before his stone lion. Bartholomeus stood beside him, pointing to some sections by the lion's eyes that he could carve more deeply. Andarius was amazed to see how clearly the lion's head stood out. He sat on a stone block near a pillar, listening to the hammering, chiselling, shouts and building noises, which seemed to form a rhythm, a kind of music that inspired him. He remembered a similar feeling when, as a general, he could see that a battle was turning in his favour. Wasn't this also a fight for victory? The victory of a divine message, which, through Vero's words, had seized him, and behind which the old Rome faded away?

He murmured to himself, *It seems as though I, too, may be on the way to becoming a Christian. Pyrra has already been to the Christian's service several times. Up to now I've firmly refused. It didn't seem appropriate for a Roman general to crawl into a cellar, to embrace a new belief. But this building speaks a language I can understand. The walls, the enclosing domed roof, all point to an inward path. With what rituals will they tend this central altar? Will the Christians be able to fill this beautiful shrine with real life?*

He was woken from these thoughts by a yell of delight from Bartholomeus, as he looked again at Milon's lion head. "Milon, you can do it! You're a born sculptor! *You* must work on the altar lion and no one else!"

Andarius stood up and went over to them. The stone lion looked at him with kingly eyes, although there was hardly anything to be seen of the mane and ears. Andarius joined in Bartholomeus' praise. It was decided: Milon would return to help work on the altar.

Milon and Andarius said little as they drove back to their estate through the dusk. The events of the day lived on in them. Before they arrived home Andarius remarked, "That was a good day in Alexandria. I'll go again to help build!"

A Slave is Also Human

Months passed. The last wood, stone and rubble were cleared away from the building site. In a few days they hoped to consecrate the space and hold the first service. Looking at the temple from the outside, everything was complete. Inside Philippus was still working on the last patch of mosaic in the dome. Over the last few weeks, Lesco had cheerfully worked with Philippus and his helpers to fix the mosaic tiles into wet mortar, high on the scaffold under the dome. This required a lot of patience and stamina, as they worked facing upwards, sometimes lying, sometimes standing. Mortar and dust trickled down and stung their eyes. Oil lamps were needed because, even during the day, it was dark inside the building. Only a pale light shone through the thin alabaster windows.

One night Vero couldn't get to sleep. He went down into the courtyard to take a walk in the night air. As he stepped out into the dark, the great, domed building loomed before him, mighty against the night sky. He noticed that an alabaster window was glowing dimly, as if a light burned inside. Had Philippus forgotten to extinguish the light when he locked up the building? Recently during the day, strangers had wandered into the courtyard in curiosity. What if someone had broken in to look at the temple or even to damage it? What if an enemy of the Christians was planning to set fire to it?

Vero approached the door cautiously. Should he wake one of his sons? Putting his ear to the wooden plank he heard a sound: yes, there was someone inside! He tried the door, but it was locked. Puzzled, he took the key from his belt and slipped it into the lock. Turning it silently, he stepped into the arched doorway. A small light burned on the scaffolding. He could hear soft singing from the domed darkness, a song without words, slow and serene. Lesco was working in the middle of the night, high up in the dome, while everyone else slept. He must have let himself be locked in, unnoticed by Philippus, so that he could continue to work.

For a moment Vero wondered whether he should call him down and send him away, but then he thought, *He loves his work so much that he goes to such pains, and even sings; I won't disturb him in his mosaic heaven.* Quietly he closed the door behind him, keeping the night's secret to himself.

A few more days and the last mosaic, a sun-like star, was fixed in place. Now the scaffolding could be removed. Philippus rushed outside to tell Vero and Marius, just as Vero came strolling across the courtyard with Milon and Baarla.

"What great timing!" cried Philippus. "The building is finished! I'm just going to fetch a few workers and Marius to help remove the frame."

Vero, Milon and Baarla stood for a moment while they became accustomed to the darkness. From the very top of the dome Lesco called down, "Milon, Baarla!" Followed, almost immediately, by a deafening noise. A beam, which had already been loosened, slipped away from Lesco's foot. He lost his balance, and with the beam, plummeted to the ground. Wood crashed to the floor in front of the altar, followed by the thud of a human body on stone paving.

"Lesco!" cried Milon and rushed to his side. He lay unmoving. Blood from his head trickled onto the stone. His eyes stared upwards, wide open. Milon knelt beside him and whispered, "Lesco, you're alive!"

Lesco's eyes turned slowly towards Milon. His lips moved. With hardly a sigh, he breathed the words, "I ... am ... a man!"

"Yes, Lesco, a good man!"

For a moment a light shone in his dying eyes, which were fixed on the gold star in the centre of the dome. Then slowly, with a last sigh, life left him.

It seemed to Milon in that moment that Lesco's soul grew larger, expanded to fill the whole building, penetrating the

pillars, shining into the gold of the mosaic star which shimmered softly down in the light of the lamp; the lamp which had lit the last work of the dead man's hands.

Baarla knelt beside Milon. With one hand she steadied herself against the stone lion of the altar before which Lesco lay, with the other she took the dead man's hand. She felt how the warmth slowly drained from it.

Vero said some words about dying in Christ and of resurrection into a spiritual life. Without intending it, their consecration of the building was beginning with a funeral.

When Philippus and Marius entered with the slaves to remove the scaffolding, they stood rooted to the spot at the scene before them: the beam, the dead man, and the kneeling figures. There was no need to explain what had happened, but they still couldn't take it in. They had all become friends with Lesco since working together. Philippus leant against one of the pillars.

One of the slaves stepped forward and asked, "Shall we bury him outside the city, as is usual with slaves?"

"A slave is also human," said Philippus. "He stays here! Bring some lights!"

At that, one of them went up the ladder to fetch Lesco's lamp from the scaffold, another brought two more, which they lit using Lesco's lamp. And so it happened that the dead man lay before the altar surrounded by lights. In their glow the scaffold beams were carried out and for the first time the bare, inner beauty of the building could be seen.

News of the accident spread quickly. Everyone who had worked on the building came, bringing flowers and green branches to honour the dead man. In the evening Vero had two paving stones lifted from the floor and a grave dug beneath them. Lesco's body was laid inside.

The following day when Vero said a blessing for the dead man, before the gathered company of Christians and builders, he ended with the words, "May our brother, Lesco, always remain with us as a good spirit of enthusiasm and work in the service of Christ."

Then Vero lit a silver lamp upon the altar and said, "Let the light of this lamp burn day and night from now on, as a symbol of eternal life."

Homeward with Hindrances

Pyrra and Baarla sat on the terrace in the garden of Andarius, stitching a white Roman bridal gown. They were so engrossed in their work that they didn't even notice Andarius come out of the house. He smiled at the silent concentration of the two women and said jokingly, "If the bride's dress isn't ready by the day after tomorrow the wedding will have to be postponed for a week!"

Baarla replied, "It's as good as ready. Before the sun sets the last stitch will be done!" She stood up, holding the dress against herself and laughed with Andarius.

"It looks splendid," he said. "Worthy of the daughter of a general! But where's the bridegroom?"

"I was about to ask," said Baarla. "Hasn't he returned from Alexandria yet?"

"No, he would have come straight here to you, of course. I don't understand why he's taking so long. He drove off very early. He wanted to run a few important errands at the market and be back in the afternoon. Now it's almost evening. Milon's usually so reliable."

There was an undertone of reproach in Andarius' words and Baarla dared not show her concern. She was afraid that something might have happened to Milon.

Andarius left and Pyrra calmed Baarla. "There's always so much to see in a big city. Maybe he stayed longer with his friends."

"But the sun will be setting soon. He promised to be back in the afternoon. It's unlike Milon to not keep his word. I hope nothing terrible has happened to him!"

Baarla's suspicions were true. Something had happened to Milon.

Milon had handed the chariot and horses to a guard in the

market by the Moon Gate, who looked after the chariots of noble customers. Later when they returned Philippus said, "Milon, the grave of the great Alexander who founded this city is close by. Would you come with me to visit his tomb? I've been wanting to see it for a long time."

"Yes, of course," Milon said. "He was a great general of Greece. Andarius told me about him. He conquered the Persian Empire and brought the light of Greece to shine here, too. "

"Yes, that's him. His tomb and sarcophagus are not far from here."

"Well, we mustn't stay too long," Milon reminded him. "I don't have much time because of the wedding preparations. Let's go!"

They soon found the famous tomb and stepped down into the underground temple where the sarcophagus stood. The four marble sides showed carved scenes of the victorious Alexander in the tumult of battle. Philippus was amazed at the beauty of the Greek sculpture.

Milon said, "Four hundred years have passed since the time of Alexander the Great. His tomb is not honoured much any more, even though he was a hero in his time. Only a few curious people stick their noses in here and soon pull them out from the mouldy darkness. Strangely, I can't help comparing this with Lesco's grave, arched over by a dome in which the living word resounds. Vero once said, 'In the light of Christ, all human beings are brothers and sisters.' Doesn't that mean Alexander and Lesco too?"

They left the dreary, sunken room thoughtfully. As they stepped outside Philippus was ready to say goodbye, intending to walk. But Milon insisted on taking him home in the chariot, as it was only a short detour. They drove through the streets of Alexandria, but it was nearly midday and the streets were so crowded that at times they had to slow to walking pace.

Jonea was in his courtyard when Milon and Philippus arrived. He called out, "The meal is nearly ready, come and be my guests!"

Of course they couldn't refuse this friendly invitation. A

slave hurried to take the horse. And this is why Milon was late, because a meal with Jonea always lasted a long time, with deep conversation.

When Milon finally left the city gates behind, he urged the horses into a gallop. Soon the city was far behind. There was no traffic on this small road during the heat of the day, so Milon could use it as a racetrack, especially since he was late. How wonderfully the horses galloped in rhythm; how refreshingly the wind brushed his bare arms and legs. He imagined himself racing with Florus in Rome. He clicked and whistled to the horses, urging them to give their best. But as he thundered down the paved track, one wheel hit a stone. A worn linchpin sprang out and, in the next instant, the wheel spun off the axle. The vehicle tipped. With a jolt Milon was flung sideways in an arch over the verge and landed on sandy ground. The horses dragged

the vehicle a short distance until it jammed into the verge. Milon lay unconscious by the roadside.

He lay unprotected in the hot sun, while the horses struggled to free themselves from their harness. At last a wagon with Roman soldiers approached from the city. They stopped, got down and lifted the unconscious Milon onto their vehicle. One of them took care of the horses. Another managed to put the wheel back onto the axle; he replaced the pin with a wooden peg, cut from an olive branch. It would do for the journey home. Milon, apart from a few grazes, showed no serious injury.

"Lucky that he didn't fall on the stone paving," said one of the soldiers.

Soon Milon awoke, wondering what had happened.

"Driving too fast?" one of the soldiers asked.

"Linchpin came out of the axle. Wheel flew off!" added another.

Milon looked at the horses to make sure they were all right. The chariot didn't seem too damaged. He thanked his helpers and asked, "Could one of you drive me to the estate of General Andarius?"

When they heard the name, famous in Alexandria, they were all eager to drive him home, hoping to receive a rich reward. Milon chose one and rewarded the others from his purse. They continued their journey at a leisurely pace. They wouldn't arrive before nightfall.

In the meantime Andarius had grown evermore restless. He ordered, "Rano, take a fast horse and ride towards Alexandria. Perhaps something's happened to him on the way." Soon dust spurted under the hooves of the messenger. Baarla tried her best to look calm and hopeful; Pyrra wailed as if *her* bridegroom was late.

Rano rode hard for around half an hour before it began to grow dark, then he had to slow his pace. Suddenly he heard the rattle of a wagon. He stopped his horse and called, "Milon!"

"Rano!" answered a familiar voice.

The story was soon told, and Milon felt much better in the

cool night air. He asked Rano for his horse, so that he could get back quickly, and he disappeared into the darkening night. He was used to riding in the dark, but he didn't hurry his horse. As he thought back to what had happened, he was grateful that the accident hadn't been worse. He could have broken his limbs, or his neck!

Specks of light glimmered in the distance, growing ever larger — the torches at the entrance of the courtyard. He knew that Baarla would be waiting. Instinctively he urged his horse on. The glimmer grew to bright flames. Dogs barked. People ran to the gate. Milon held Baarla close.

Inside by lamplight she spread ointment on his grazes, smiled, and said, "Milon, that time in the stall when I tended your wounds, I had no idea that later I'd be doing it again as your bride."

"Baarla, even small wounds will always remind us that our love began in suffering."

Outside they heard the rumble of the chariot, which Andarius was waiting for impatiently. He wanted to check the wheels. He couldn't understand how *his* chariot had lost a pin. He examined the vehicle and gave orders to forge new linchpins for every carriage on the estate the very next day.

With Song and Dance

The days leading up to Milon and Baarla's wedding were filled with busy preparations. The Veros had offered to plan the wedding ceremony. Until now there had been no such Christian custom. So they discussed how they could bless the couple before the altar. The Christians in Alexandria, who had gathered to help build the temple, asked old father Vero to become one of their priests. As he tried to decide whether he could accept this offer, Vero remembered how the hand of the apostle Paul had rested on his head when Paul had baptised and blessed him in Rome. And he thought, *With the help of this blessing I will try to serve at the altar.*

So he gave his consent and prepared to celebrate the coming wedding. Dina practised an altar dance for days with some of the young girls. Marius finished the great lyre, which he had begun to make some time ago, so that they'd have string music. Philippus and Bartholomeus gathered a choir together to practise songs in harmony.

When the day finally came, Andarius and Pyrra drove to Alexandria with Milon and Baarla, their carriage wreathed in leaves and flowers. Songs rose up to greet them as they entered the door of the domed temple. The choir of twelve men stood in a circle with burning candles before the pillars. Between them were the young dancers, with flowers in their hands. Behind stood the circle of Christian friends and guests. The couple approached the altar, where the bread and chalice lay on either side of the silver lamp.

Vero, in his long white priest's robe, received the bride and groom with open arms. He took them both by the hand, Milon to his right and Baarla to his left. With songs and incense filling the temple, the twelve young girls stepped forward to begin their solemn ring dance. In the candlelight that reflected from the gold stars above, they danced to the notes of the lyre. Such a powerful sense of inner joy arose in everyone's heart that you would think they were all in Paradise.

The singing faded, the ring dance slowed and they all stood still.

Vero raised his voice: "Peace be with us, dear brothers and sisters! Here on earth, right amongst us, miracles occur. We only need to keep our eyes open to notice them. Here at my right stands Milon. In fear and despair he was once carried over the sea to Rome, to face a cruel death. But wise guidance has led him to freedom, a new life and true friends. He has become our brother. Next to him stands Baarla. As a young child she lost her mother who, before she died, blessed her in the name of Christ. The spark of that blessing continued to shine in her. As a faithful servant she has quietly done her work. Where she could help she did so, always remembering the words, 'Love your neighbour as yourself.' Now these two stand before the altar and I join their hands together, as a sign that they shall be united in life and in following after Christ!"

As Vero's words ended, the choir began to sing. The young girls brought their flowers to the couple. Then, with only the soft tones of the lyre sounding, the community stepped to the altar beside the couple to receive the holy bread and wine together.

When the celebration had ended Jonea proclaimed, "My house is ready! You're all invited to be my guests. Come and feast at my table!"

As Milon and Baarla were about to leave through the great arched door, Milon turned back towards the altar. "Father Vero," he said, "you told me once that Mark was a disciple of the Lord and proclaimed the gospel, and that the lion was his sign. So far our temple has had no name. Could it be called the Temple of Mark? It was a real, earthly lion who guided us here, towards the heavenly lion."

Old Vero's face lit up with joy. "I've been waiting for the day when the right name would come to me," he exclaimed. "And here it is! Milon and Baarla, step out into your new life together, through the gate of the Temple of Mark!"

And as they walked out into the brilliant Egyptian sunshine, followed by Vero, a rain of roses showered upon them — from the children, who had filled their baskets with flowers — turning the quiet festival into one of delight, happiness and laughter.